She was not the only one there.

I'm the only one here, Nicoletta told herself. I must stop screaming.

She was wrong.

She was not the only one there.

The cave filled with movement and smell and she was picked up, actually held in the air, by whatever else was in the cave with her.

A creature from that other, lower, darker world.

Its skin rasped against hers like saw grass. Its stink was unbreathable. Its hair was dead leaves, crisping against each other and breaking off in her face. Warts of sand covered it, and the sand actually came off on her, as if the creature were half made out of the cave itself.

She could not see any of the thing, only feel and smell it.

It was holding her, as if in an embrace.

**Other books by Caroline B. Cooney
you will enjoy:**

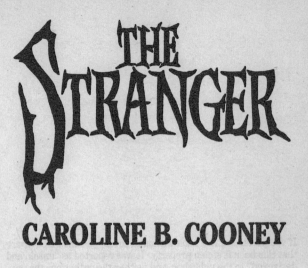

THE STRANGER

CAROLINE B. COONEY

SCHOLASTIC INC.
New York Toronto London Auckland Sydney

No part of this publication may be reproduced in whole or in part, or stored in a retrieval system, or transmitted in any form or by any means, electronic, mechanical, photocopying, recording, or otherwise, without written permission of the publisher. For information regarding permission, write to Scholastic Inc., 730 Broadway, New York, NY 10003.

ISBN 0-590-45680-6

12 11 10 9 8 7 6 5 4 3 2 1   3 4 5 6 7 8/9

Printed in the U.S.A.   01

First Scholastic printing, November 1993

THE STRANGER

Chapter 1

It was cold in the music room. Somebody had cracked the windows to freshen the stale school air. But Nicoletta had not expected her entire life to be chilled by the drafts of January.

"Nickie," said the music teacher, smiling a bright, false smile. Nicoletta hated nicknames but she smiled back anyway. "I called you in separately because this may be a blow. I want you to learn the news here, and not in the hallway in front of the others."

Nicoletta could not imagine what Ms. Quincy was talking about. Yesterday, tryouts for Madrigal Singers had been completed. Ms. Quincy required the members to audition every September and January, even though there was no question as to which sixteen would be chosen. Nicoletta, of course, as she had been for two years, would be one of the four sopranos.

So her first thought was that somebody was

hurt, and Ms. Quincy was breaking it to her. In a childlike gesture of which she was unaware, Nicoletta's hand caught the left side of her hair and wound it around her throat. The thick, shining gold turned into a comforting rope.

"The new girl," said Ms. Quincy. "Anne-Louise." Ms. Quincy looked at the chalkboard on which a music staff had been drawn. "She's wonderful," said Ms. Quincy. "I'm putting her in Madrigals. You have a good voice, and you're a solid singer, Nickie. Certainly a joy to have in any group. But . . . Anne-Louise has had voice lessons for years."

Nicoletta came close to strangling herself with the rope of her own yellow hair. Madrigals? The chorus into which she had poured her life? The chorus that toured the state, whose concerts were standing room only? The sixteen who were best friends? Who partied and carpooled and studied together as well as sang?

"I'm sorry," said Ms. Quincy. She looked sorry, too. She looked, to use an old and stupid phrase, as if this hurt her more than it hurt Nicoletta. "Since each part is limited to four singers, I cannot have both of you. Anne-Louise will take your place."

The wind of January crept through the one-inch window opening and iced her life. How could she could go on with high school if she were dropped from Madrigals? She had no activity but singing. Her only friends were in Madrigals.

I'll be alone, thought Nicoletta.

A flotilla of lonely places appeared in her mind: cafeteria, bus, hallway, student center.

Her body humiliated her. She became a prickly mass of perspiration: Sweaty hands, lumpy throat, tearful eyes. "Doesn't it count," she said desperately, trying to marshall intelligent arguments, "that I have never missed a rehearsal? I've never been late? I've been in charge of refreshments? I'm the one who finds ushers for the concerts and the one who checks the spelling in the programs?"

"And we'd love to have you keep doing that," said Ms. Quincy. Her smile opened again like a zipper separating her face halves.

For two years Nicoletta had idolized Ms. Quincy. Now an ugly puff of hatred filled her heart instead. "I'm not good enough to sing with you," she cried out, "but you'd love to have me do the secretarial work? I'm sure Anne-Louise has had lessons in that, too. Thanks for nothing, Ms. Quincy!"

Nicoletta ran out of the music room before she broke down into sobbing and had the ultimate humiliation of being comforted by the very woman who was kicking her out. There had been no witnesses yet, but in a few minutes everybody she cared about would know. She, Nicoletta, was not good enough anymore. The standards had been raised.

Nicoletta was just another ordinary soprano.

Nicoletta was out.

There was a narrow turn of hall between the music rooms and the lobby. Nicoletta stood in the dark silence of that space, trying to control her emotions. She could hear familiar laughter — Madrigal friends coming to read the list of the chosen. She thought suddenly of her costume: the lovely crimson gown with the tight waist and the white lace high at the throat, the tiny crown that sat in her yellow hair. People said that the medieval look suited her, that she was beautiful in red. And beautiful she always felt, spun gold, with an angel's voice.

Ms. Quincy followed her into the safety zone of the dark little hall. "Go down to Guidance, now, Nickie," she said in a teachery voice. "Sign up for something else in the Madrigal time slot."

I'll sign up for Bomb-Making, thought Nicoletta. Or Arson.

She did not look at Ms. Quincy again. She walked in the opposite direction from the known voices, taking the long way around the school to Guidance. In this immense high school, with its student body of over two thousand, she was among strangers. You had to find your place in such a vast school, and her place had been Madrigals. With whom would she stand now? With whom would she laugh and eat and gossip?

Of course in the Guidance office they pretended to be busy and Nicoletta had to sit forty minutes until they could fit her in. The chair was orange plastic, hideous and cold, the same color as the repulsive orange kitchen counters in Nicoletta's repulsive new house.

Her parents had gotten in too deep financially. Last autumn, amid tears and recrimination, the Storms family had had to sell the wonderful huge house on Fairest Hill. Oh, how Nicoletta had loved that house! Immense rooms, expanses of windows, layers of decks, acres of closets! She and her mother had poured themselves into decorating it, occupying every shopping hour with the joys of wallpaper, curtains, and accessories.

Now they were in a tiny ranch with ugly, crowded rooms, and Nicoletta was sharing a bedroom with her eleven-year-old sister, Jamie.

In their old house, Jamie had had her own bedroom and bath; Jamie had had three closets just for herself; Jamie had had her own television and *two* extra beds, so she could have sleepovers every weekend.

The ranch house had only two bedrooms, so now Jamie slept exactly six feet from Nicoletta. The seventy-two most annoying inches in the world. Nicoletta had actually liked her sister when they lived in the big house. Now the girls could do nothing except bicker, bait, and fight.

Fairest Hill.

Nicoletta always thought the name came from the fairy tale of Snow White: *Mirror, mirror, on the wall, who is the fairest of them all?*

And in those pretty woods, on top of that gentle sloping hill in that lovely house, she, Nicoletta, had been the fairest of them all.

Now she could not even sing soprano.

It was difficult to know who made her maddest — her parents, for poor planning; the economy, for making it worse; Ms. Quincy, for being rotten, mean, and cruel; or Anne-Louise, for moving here.

Within a few minutes, however, it was the guidance counselor making her maddest. "Let's see," said Mr. Parsons. "The available half-year classes, Nicoletta, are Art Appreciation, Study Skills, Current Events, and Oceanography." He skimmed through her academic files. "I certainly recommend Study Skills," he said severely.

She hated him. I'm not taking Current Events, she thought, because I sit through television news every night from five to seven as it is. I'm not taking Oceanography because deep water is the scariest thing on earth. I'm not taking Study Skills just because he thinks I should. Which leaves Art Appreciation. Art for the nonartistic. Art for the pathetic and left-behind.

"I'm signing you up for Study Skills," said Mr. Parsons.

"No. Art Appreciation."

"If you insist," said Mr. Parsons.

She insisted.

That night, as a break in the fighting with Jamie, Nicoletta received three phone calls from other Madrigal singers.

Rachel, her sidekick, the other first soprano next to whom she had stood for two lovely years was crying. "This is so awful!" she sobbed. "Doesn't Ms. Quincy understand friendship? Or loyalty? Or anything?"

Cathy, an alto so low she sometimes sang tenor, was furious. "I'm in favor of boycotting Madrigals," said Cathy. "That will teach Ms. Quincy a thing or two."

Christo, the lowest bass, and handsomest boy, also phoned.

Everybody, at one time or another, had had a crush on Christopher Hannon. Christopher had grown earlier than most boys: At fifteen he had looked twenty, and now at seventeen he looked twenty-five. He was broad-shouldered and tall and could have grown a beard to his chest had he wanted to. Nicoletta was always surprised that she and Christo were the exact same age.

"Nickie," said Christo, "this is terrible. We've all argued with Ms. Quincy. She's sick, that's what I say. Demented."

Nicoletta felt marginally better. At least her friends had stood by her and perhaps would get Ms. Quincy to change her mind and dump this horrible Anne-Louise.

"I have to take Art Appreciation instead," she said glumly.

Christo moaned. "Duds," he told her.

"I know."

"Be brave. We'll rescue you. This Anne-Louise cannot possibly sing like you, Nickie."

She entered the Art Appreciation room the following day feeling quite removed from the pathetic specimens supposed to be her class-mates. Christo, Cathy, Rachel, and her other

8

friends would turn this nightmare around. In a day or so she'd be back rehearsing like always, with a cowed and apologetic Ms. Quincy.

Without interest, Nicoletta took her new text and its companion workbook and sat where she was told, in the center of the room.

A quick survey of the other students told her she had laid eyes on none of these kids before. It was not a large class, perhaps twenty, half boys, which surprised her a little. Did they really want to appreciate art, or were they, too, refusing to take Study Skills?

The teacher, a Mr. Marisson, of whom she had never even heard let alone met, showed slides. Nicoletta prepared to go to sleep, which was her usual response to slides.

But as the room went dark, and the kids around her became shadows of themselves, her eye was caught not by the van Gogh or the Monet painting on the screen but by the profile of the boy in front of her, one row to her left.

He had the most mobile face she had ever seen. Even in the dusk of the quiet classroom, she could see him shift his jaw, lower and lift his eyes, tighten and relax his lips. Several times he lifted a hand to touch his cheek, and he touched it in a most peculiar fashion — as if he were exploring it. As if it belonged to somebody else, or as if he had not known, until this very second, that he even had a cheek.

She was so fascinated she could hardly wait for the slide show to end.

"Well, that's the end of today's lecture," said Mr. Marisson, flipping the lights back on.

The boy remained strangely dark. It was as if he cast his own shadow in his own space. His eyelashes seemed to shade his cheeks, and his cheeks seemed full of hollows. His hair was thick and fell onto his face, sheltering him from stares.

Nicoletta, who had never had an art-type thought in her life, wanted to paint him.

How weird! she thought. Maybe Mr. Marisson put him in the class just to inspire us. Perhaps this is how van Gogh and Monet got started, emotionally moved by a stranger's beautiful profile.

Never had the word *stranger* seemed so apt. There was something genuinely strange about the boy. Essentially different. But what was it?

Nicoletta could not see straight into his eyes. He kept them lowered. Not as if he were shy but as if he had other things to look at than his surroundings.

Class ended.

People stood.

Nicoletta watched the boy. He did not look

her way nor anybody else's. He did not seem aware of anyone. He left the room with a lightness of step that did not fit his body: His body was more like Christo's, yet his walk might have been a dancer's.

Nicoletta rarely initiated friendships. She tended to let friendship come to her, and it always had: through classmates or seatmates, through group lessons or neighbors. But she wanted to look into this boy's eyes, and unless she spoke to him she would not have the privilege.

Privilege? she thought. What a strange word to use! What do I mean by that? "Hi," she said to his departing back. "I'm Nicoletta."

The boy did not register her voice. He did not turn. He might have been deaf. Perhaps he was deaf. Perhaps that was his mystery; his closure from the rest. Perhaps he really was hidden away inside his silent mind.

She stopped walking but he did not.

In a few moments he vanished from sight, blending with crowds and corridors.

After school, Nicoletta saw Christo, Cathy, Rachel, and several of the others. She ran up to them. They would have spoken to Ms. Quincy again. She could hardly wait for their report.

"Hey, Nickie," said Christo. He rubbed her

shoulders and kissed her hair. Affection came easily to Christo. He distributed it to all the girls and they in turn were never without a smile or a kiss for him. But that was all there was. Christo never offered more, and never took more.

Nor did he say a word about the first Madrigal rehearsal in which Anne-Louise, and not Nicoletta, sang soprano.

"So?" said Nicoletta teasingly, keeping her voice light. She was mostly talking to Rachel, her sidekick. Her fellow sufferer in soprano jokes. (Question: A hundred dollars is lying on the ground. Who takes it — the dumb soprano or the smart soprano? Answer: The dumb soprano, of course. There's no such thing as a smart soprano.)

Rachel looked uncomfortable.

Cathy looked embarrassed.

Even Christo, who was never nervous, looked nervous.

Finally Rachel made a confused gesture with her hands, like birds fluttering. Awkwardly, she mumbled, "Anne-Louise is really terrific, Nicoletta. She has the best voice of any of us. She is — well — she's — " Rachel seemed unable to think of what else Anne-Louise might be.

"She's Olympic material," said Christo.

Rachel managed giggles. "There's no soprano divison in the Olympics, Christo."

But it was very clear. Anne-Louise was miles better than Nicoletta. Nicoletta was not going to get back in. She was not going to be a Madrigal again. Her friends had put no arguments before Ms. Quincy.

"But come with us to Keyboard, Nickie," said Rachel quickly. "There's so much to talk about. You have to tell us about Art Appreciation. I mean, is it wall-to-wall duds, or what?"

Keyboard was the city's only ice-cream parlor with a piano. Perhaps the world's only ice-cream parlor with a piano. For years and years, before Nicoletta was even born, the high school Madrigals had hung out there, singing whenever they felt like it. They sang current hits and ancient tunes, they sang Christmas carols and kindergarten rounds, they sang rock or country or sixteenth-century love songs. In between, they had sundaes, milk shakes, or Cokes, and stuck quarters in the old-fashioned jukebox with its glittering lights and dated music.

Okay, thought Nicoletta, trying to breathe, trying to accept the slap in the face of Anne-Louise's superiority. We're still friends, I can still —

Anne-Louise joined the group.

She was an ordinary-looking girl, with dull brown hair and small brown eyes. But the other singers did not look at her as if *they* saw anything ordinary. They were full of admiration.

She'll wear my crimson gown, thought Nicoletta. She'll put my sparkling crown in her plain hair. She'll sing my part.

Christo rubbed Anne-Louise's shoulders and kissed her hair exactly as he had Nicoletta's. Anne-Louise bit her lip with embarrassment and pleasure, and said, "Are you sure you want me along?"

"Of course we do!" the rest chorused. "You're a Madrigal now."

And I'm not, thought Nicoletta.

Rachel and Cathy protested, but Nicoletta did not go to Keyboard with them. She claimed she had to help her mother at home. They knew it was a lie, but it certainly made things easier for everybody. With visible gratitude, the new arrangement of Madrigals left in their new lineup.

Nicoletta headed for the school bus, which she rarely took. Christo had a van and usually ferried Madrigals wherever he went. But she did not get on the bus after all.

Walking purposefully down the road, knowing his destination, was the dark and silent boy from Art Appreciation.

The high school was not located for walking home. It had been built a decade ago in a rural area, so that it could be wrapped in playing fields of the most impressive kind. No student lived within walking distance. Yellow buses awaiting their loads snaked around two roads, slowly filling with kids from every corner of the city.

Yet the boy walked.

And Nicoletta, because she was lost, followed him.

Chapter 2

The first two blocks of following the boy meant nothing; anybody could reasonably walk down the wide cement.

But then the boy turned, and strode down a side street, stepping on every frozen puddle and cracking its ice. DEAD END said the sign at the top of the street. Nicoletta had never even noticed the street. The boy surely knew everybody on his street, and he would also know that she did not live there, had no business walking there. That she had no destination at the DEAD END.

At no other moment in her life would she have continued. Nicoletta was conventional. She was comfortable with social rules and did not break them, nor care to be around people who did.

But all the rules of her life had been broken that day. She had lost her circle, her pleasure.

She had been found lacking, and not only that, she had been replaced by someone better.

The sick humiliation in her heart was so painful that she found herself distanced from the world. The rules were hard to remember and not meaningful when she did remember them. She was facing a terrible empty time in which the group she loved forgot her. If she filled the time by going home, she'd have a crabby sister, a small house, and a nervous mother. She'd have television reruns played too loud, a fattening snack she didn't need, and homework she couldn't face.

So Nicoletta crossed the road, and followed the boy down the little lane.

She had his attention now. An odd, keep-your-back-turned attention. He didn't look around at her. At one point he paused, and stood very still. She matched him. He walked on; she walked on. He walked faster for a while; she did, too. Then he slowed down. So did Nicoletta.

Her head and mind felt light and airy. She felt as if she might faint, or else fly away.

She was mesmerized by the task of making her feet land exactly when his did. He had long strides. She could not possibly cover as much ground. She was carrying her books, hugging them in her arms, and they grew heavy. She hardly noticed. Her head was swimming and there was nothing in the universe but the rhythm of their walking.

The houses ended.

The road narrowed.

The trees that had neatly stayed inside hedges and yards now arched over the street. Latticed, bare branches fenced off the sky. In summer this would be a green tunnel. In winter it was grim and mean.

The asphalt ended. The road became dirt ruts.

Nicoletta would have said there were no dirt roads in the entire state, let alone this city. Where could the boy be going?

Trees grew as closely as fence posts. Prickly vines wrapped the edge of the woods as viciously as concertina wire. Stone walls threaded through the naked woods, the lost farms of early America. For a moment, she felt their souls: the once-breathing farmers, the vanished field hands, the dead wives, and buried children.

At the end of the dirt lane, an immense boulder loomed like a huge altar from some old-world circle of stones.

Nicoletta had the strangest sensation that the stone greeted the boy. That the stone, not the boy, changed expression. They knew each other.

Nicoletta kept coming.

Some boys would have readied for combat. They would have slipped into the athletic stance used for obstructing or catching. This boy was simply there.

Very, very slowly he turned to see whose feet had been matching his, what person had trespassed on his road. Dark motionless eyes, falling heavy hair, smooth quiet features. Not a word. Not a gesture.

People often asked Nicoletta if her shining gold hair was really hers. They often asked her if her vivid green eyes were really hers. The general assumption was that extremely blonde hair and very green eyes must be the result of dye and contact lenses. She hated being asked if parts of her body were really hers.

And yet she wanted to ask this boy — *Is that really you*? There was something so different about him. As if he wore a mask to be pulled off.

There were about twenty paces between them. Neither he nor she attempted to narrow the distance.

"Hi," she said at last. She struggled for a smile, but fear gave her a twitch instead.

He did not ask her what she was doing, nor where she was going.

"I followed you," she said finally.

He nodded.

A flush of shame rose up on her face. She was a fool. She was utterly pathetic. "It was just something to do," she offered him.

Still his face did not move.

She struggled to find explanations for her ridiculous behavior. "I had a bad day. I lost all my friends. So — you were walking — and I walked, too — and here we are."

His face did not change.

"Where's your house?" she said desperately.

At last he spoke. But he did not tell her where his house was. He said softly, "You can't have lost *all* your friends." His voice was like butter: soft and golden. She loved his voice.

"No," she agreed. "Probably not. It just feels like it. It turns out I'm not as important as I thought."

He said, "I'll walk you back to the road while you tell me about it."

She told him about it.

He simply nodded. His expression never changed. It was neither friendly nor hostile, neither sorry for her nor annoyed with her. He was just there. She wondered what his mouth would look like smiling. What his mouth would feel like kissing.

Nicoletta talked.

He listened.

She poured out her feelings as if he were her psychiatric counselor and she was paying by the hour. She had to face this boy tomorrow, and every day for the rest of the school year! And yet here she was describing the workings of her heart and soul, as if he were a friend, as if he could be trusted.

It was horrifically cold. She had not worn clothing for a hike in the outdoors. She shifted her books, trying to wrap her cold hands inside one another.

The boy took off his long scarf, which was plain, thin black wool, with no fringe and no pattern. He wrapped it gently around her freezing ears, brought the ends down and tucked them around her icy fingers. The wool was warm with his heat. She wanted to have the scarf forever.

She had to know more about him. She wanted to see him with his family, standing in his yard. She wanted to see him in his car and in his kitchen. She wanted to see him wearing jeans and wearing bathing trunks.

"Will you be able to get home from here?" he asked instead. They were standing next to the bright yellow DEAD END sign. A few hundred yards ahead, traffic spun its endless circuit.

She could not let their time together end. In fact, standing with him, they did not seem to be in normal time; they were in some other time; a wide, spacious ancient time. "Were you just going for a hike or do you live down there?" Nicoletta said.

He regarded her steadily. "It's a shortcut," he said finally.

He's very, very rich, thought Nicoletta. He lives on an immense estate by the ocean. Acres of farm and forest between us and his circular drive. Perhaps his mother is a famous movie star and they live under another name. She said, "I'm Nicoletta Storms."

"Nicoletta," he repeated. How softly he sounded each consonant. How romantic and European it sounded on his lips. Antique and lyrical. Not the way her classmates said it, getting the long name over with. Or switching without permission to Nickie.

"What's your name?" she said.

For a while she thought he would not tell her; that even giving out his name to a classmate was too much personal expression for him. Then he said, "Jethro."

"Jethro?" she repeated. "What an odd name!

Are you named for an ancestor?"

He actually smiled. She was lifted up on that smile like a swallow on a gust of summer wind. His smile was beautiful; it was wonderful; it was buried treasure, and she, Nicoletta, had uncovered it.

Their city was one of the oldest on the East Coast. She had never previously met a native, but there had to be some. Perhaps Jethro was a descendant of the *Mayflower*. That was the kind of name they gave boys back then. Jethro, Truth, Ephraim.

"Ancestors," he agreed. The smile slowly closed, leaving behind only a sweet friendliness.

"How did you like Art Appreciation?" she said. She did not want to stop talking. "Do you know a lot about art or were the slides new to you?"

"Everything is new to me," the boy answered, and gave away the first tiny clue. Slightly, he emphasized *everything*. As if not just art were new — but everything. The world.

"Let's have lunch together tomorrow," she said.

He stared at her, eyes and mouth flaring in astonishment. And blushed. "Lunch," repeated Jethro, as if unfamiliar with it.

"Meet me in the cafeteria?" said Nicoletta. She wanted to kiss him. Rachel would have. Rachel would have stood on her tiptoes, leaned forward, and kissed long and slow, even the first time. Rachel felt kissing was the world's best hallway activity. Teachers were always telling Rachel to chill out.

Instead the boy touched her face with his fingertips.

And Nicoletta, indeed, chilled.

It was not the hand of a human.

Chapter 3

"Of course he's a human," said her sister Jamie. Jamie was absolutely disgusted with the end of the story. "Nick, you blew it. I cannot believe you turned around and ran!" Jamie was always convinced that she would handle any situation whatsoever a hundred times better than her older sister. Here was yet more proof.

Nicoletta hated defending herself to a child of eleven. But it happened constantly. There was no decision Nicoletta made, including, of course, being born, which met with her sister's approval. "I was scared."

Jamie flung up her hands in exasperation. "If you had enough guts to follow him into the dark and dank and dreary woods . . ."

"They weren't dark or dank or dreary. The sun was shining. There was still snow on the ground in the forest. It was more silver than dark."

"My *point*," said Jamie, with the immense disgust of younger sisters who were going to get things *right* when *they* started dating, "is that he started talking to you! Flirting with you. You even invited him to meet you for lunch. Running away from him was stupid, stupid, stupid, stupid, stupid."

Their father said, "Jamie. Please. You are entitled to your opinion, but saying it once is enough."

The worst thing about this minihouse was the way they had to function in each other's laps. There was no privacy. All conversations and confrontations became family property. Nicoletta thought of their lovely house on Fairest Hill, and how she should have had an entire suite in which to be alone and consider her — well, Jamie was right — her stupidity.

"Besides," said their mother, "of course the boy's hands were cold. You'd been in the woods for hours and he didn't have any gloves on and it's January." Mother sniffed. She did not like fantasy, and when the girls were quite small, and liked to make things up, their mother put a stop to it in a hurry. "Not human," repeated Mrs. Storms irritably. "Really, Nicoletta."

Nicoletta had told them about Jethro because it was easier than telling them about Madrigals. She could not bring herself to say that part out loud. *I'm not in it anymore. You won't go to concerts anymore. You won't have to iron my beautiful medieval gown ever again. Somebody else — somebody named Anne-Louise — gets to dress up and sing like an angel and hear the applause from now on.*

"Speaking as the only man in this family, . . ." said Nicoletta's father. He looked long and carefully at his hands, as if reading the backs instead of the palms. "I want to say that if some girl followed me home, walked after me for miles through the woods, and told me she had a crush on me, and then I walked her all the way back to the main road, I would certainly have been hoping for a kiss. And if instead of throwing her arms around me, the girl *fled* . . . well, Nickie, I would feel I'd done something incredibly stupid or had turned out to be repulsive close up. I'd want to change schools in the morning. I'd never want to have to face that girl again."

Wonderful, thought Nicoletta, wanting to weep. Now I'll never see him again.

She struggled with tears. In the other house, she could have wept alone. In this one, she had witnesses. The small-minded part of her tried to hold her parents responsible, and hate them instead of herself, for being a complete dummy and running from Jethro.

She remembered the cold touch of his hands. I don't care what Mother says, thought Nicoletta. Jethro's hands were not normal. He scared me. There really was something strange about him. Something terribly wrong, something not quite of this world. I felt it through his skin. I can still feel it. Even though I have washed my hands, I can still feel it.

"So," said her father, his voice changing texture, becoming rich and teasing, "what'll we do tonight, Nickie? Want me to play my fiddle?"

Jamie got right into it. Nothing brought her more satisfaction than annoying her big sister. "Or we could slice up a turnip," Jamie agreed. "That would be fun."

Right up until high school, Nicoletta had loved the *Little House* books. How unfair that she had to live now where the family could go to McDonald's if they got hungry, check out a video if they got bored, and turn the thermostat up if they got chilled. A younger Nicoletta had prayed every night to fall through a time warp and arrive on the banks of Plum Creek with Mary and Laura. She wanted a covered wagon and a sod house and, of course, she wanted to meet Almanzo and marry him. In middle school, Nicoletta had decided to learn everything Laura had to learn; quilting, pie making, knitting, stomping on hay. Nicoletta's mother, who hated needlework and bought frozen pies, could not stand it. "You live in the twentieth century and that's that. Ma Ingalls," Nicoletta's mother said, "would have been thrilled to live like you. Warm in winter, snow never coming through the cracks, fresh fruit out of season."

When she was Jamie's age, Nicoletta had made her fatal error. "Daddy never gets out his fiddle and sings songs for me when it's snowing outside," she'd said.

Her father laughed for years. He was always making fiddle jokes.

The second fatal error came shortly after, when Nicoletta tried eating raw sliced turnip because the Ingalls considered it a snack. Nicoletta's mother had never in her life even bought a turnip because, she said, "Even the word gives me indigestion."

Only last Christmas, Nicoletta's stocking had included a raw turnip and a paring knife. "Instead of potato chips," said the card. "Love from Santa on the Prairie." It was Jamie's handwriting.

Nicoletta's *Little House* obsession ended with Madrigals: The singing, the companionship of a wonderful set of boys and girls from tenth to twelfth grade, the challenge of memorizing the difficult music filled Nicoletta the way her pioneer fantasies once had.

She thought of her life as divided by these two: the *Little House* daydream years and the Madrigal reality years.

And now Madrigals were over.

She was not a Madrigal singer. She was just another soprano, good enough only for the ordinary non-audition chorus.

Unwillingly, Nicoletta looked at the photograph of herself on the mantel. Every few years these photos were replaced, when the old one began to seem dated and ridiculous. Nicoletta's portrait had been taken only last fall, and she stood slim and beautiful in her long satin skirt, crimson fabric cascading from her narrow waist, white lace like sea froth around her slender throat. Her yellow hair had just been permed, and twisted like ribbons down to her shoulders. In her hair glittered a thread of jewels. She seemed like a princess from another age, another continent, dressed as a Nicoletta should be dressed.

Now she hated the portrait. People would come to the house — Rachel, Cathy, Christo — and there it would sit, pretending nothing had changed.

I don't want this life! thought Nicoletta, her throat filling with a detestable lump. Who needs high school? It hurts too much. I don't measure up. I'm not musical and I'm a jerk who runs away from boys and makes them wish they attended school in another town. I don't care what my mother says. Laura Ingalls had it good. Blizzards, starvation, three-hundred-mile hikes, scary badgers, and flooding creeks.

She thought of Jethro. His profile. His odd, silent darkness. His quiet listening while she poured out her pain.

"I got kicked out of Madrigals," Nicoletta said abruptly. "Ms. Quincy tried everybody out again, and a new girl named Anne-Louise is better than I am, so I'm out and she's in and I don't want to talk about it."

Chapter 4

She did not dream of Madrigals.

She dreamed of Jethro.

When she awoke much earlier than usual it was quickly and cleanly, with none of the usual muddleheaded confusion of morning. She arose swiftly and dressed without worry.

That in itself amazed Nicoletta. Choosing clothing normally took her half an hour the night before, and then in the morning half an hour to decide that last night's choice would not do, and yet another half hour to find clothing that would fit the day after all. It was amazing how an outfit that had been absolutely the right choice for last Thursday was never the right choice for the following Thursday.

She did not brush her hair; Nicoletta's permed curls were too tight for a brush to manage. She ran her fingers through it, fluffing and smoothing at the same time. She put on a simple black turtleneck, a plain silver necklace, and narrow dangling silver earrings. She wore a skirt she rarely touched: It had two layers, a tight black sheath covered by a swirl of filmy black gauze. The skirt was dressy, but the plain turtleneck brought it down to school level.

She did not look romantic. She looked as if she were in mourning. For Madrigals? Or for the boy she would not meet for lunch after all?

Jethro.

Her school bus did not pass the strange little country lane she had never before noticed. When she got off the bus, she looked for him, but she had never seen him wandering around the school before, and she did not see him now. In the halls, her eyes scanned the taller people, searching for him, both aching and scared that she would actually spot him.

First-period history, she covered a page in her notebook with the name Jethro. It looked historical. Where did it come from? It sounded Biblical. Who was Jethro and what had he done? She wrote it in script, in plain print, in decorated print, in open block letters. She wrote it backhand and she wrote it billboard style, enclosed in frames.

Second-period English, the other person in her life with an O name sat beside her. Christo. "Hi, Nick," he said cheerfully.

She had always admired Christopher's endless cheer. It seemed an admirable way to face life: ever up, ever smiling, ever optimistic and happy.

Now it seemed shallow. Annoying.

Am I comparing him to Jethro or am I angry with him for still being in Madrigals, for making peace in a single day with the fact that I have been replaced? "Hi, Christo," she said. He had not even noticed how she skipped a beat before answering him.

The teacher had visited England last year and, sad to say, taken along his camera and several million rolls of film. Today he had yet more slides of where famous English authors had lived and gone to college and gardened. It was the gardening that most amazed Nicoletta. Who could possibly care what flowers bloomed in the gardens that no longer belonged to the famous — and now dead — authors? In fact, who could possibly have cared back when the famous authors were alive?

Nicoletta sat quietly while the teacher bustled — fixing his slides, flipping switches, lowering screens, focusing.

Christo murmured in her ear. "Nicoletta?"

His use of her whole name startled her. She turned to look at him, but his face was so close to her they touched cheeks instead.

"There's a dance Friday," whispered Christo. "I know it's late to be asking, but would you go with me?"

Nicoletta was stunned. Christo? Who showed affection to everybody equally? Christo, who never appeared to notice whether he was patting the shoulder of Nicoletta or Rachel or Cathy, or — now — Anne-Louise? Christo, for whom girls seemed to be just one generic collection of the opposite sex?

Christo. Who was certainly the best-looking and most-yearned-for boy in school.

She absolutely knew for a fact that Christo had never had a date.

One of the things Madrigals spared you was dating. You had your crowd; you had your portable group. You had people with whom to laugh and share pizza. Rarely did any of them pair up, either within or without the group.

On the big white screen at the front of the class, appeared a dazzling slide from inside a cathedral. Great gray stones held up a gleaming and terrifying stained glass window. The glass people were in primary colors: scarlet arms, blue gowns, golden heads. If Jethro were hers, she, too, would be as vivid as that: Together they would blind the eye.

If I go to a dance with Christo, how can

Jethro ask me out? Nicoletta thought. I want to be with Jethro.

Christo's hand covered hers. She dropped her eyes, and then her whole head, staring down at his hand. His hand was afraid. She could feel uncertainty in the way he touched her. Christo, who touched everybody without ever thinking of it, or knowing he was doing it, was fearful of touch.

The slide changed and a gargoyle appeared on the screen. Carved stone. An unknowable man-creature stared out from oak leaves that were both his hair and his beard, which grew into him and, at the same time, grew out of him. *It's Jethro*, thought Nicoletta.

"That sounds wonderful," she murmured, mostly to Christo's hand. "I'd love to go. What dance is it?"

"Fund-raiser," said Christo. "It'll be at Top o' the Town."

A famous restaurant where in years past her father had taken her mother for special occasions, like Valentine's Day or their anniversary. Nicoletta had never been there. It was not a place that people wasted on children.

I'm not a child, thought Nicoletta. I'm a young woman, and Christo knows it. Christo wants me. He doesn't want any of the others.

Not Rachel or Cathy. And not this Anne-Louise. But me.

She looked nervously at Christo in the half-dark of the classroom. He was truly nervous. His easy smile puckered in and out. He had needed the dark to do this; he had chosen a place where they could not possibly continue the conversation or else people would hear, and because lights would come on in a moment, and the teacher would begin his lecture.

She was amazed at the discovery that Christo was afraid of anything at all, let alone her.

But when she looked at him, she still saw Jethro.

Who is Jethro? thought Nicoletta, that he has consumed me. Who am I, that I am letting it happen? Mother is right; daydreaming and fantasy are silly and only lead to silly choices. I'll stop right now.

Then came chemistry.
Then came French.
Then came lunch.
And Jethro was there.

He had come. He was waiting. He did mean to meet her.

She saw him from far across the room. Her whole body shivered, and she did not understand him the way she had to her surprise understood Christo. She could not imagine who that person Jethro was. He was as hidden to her as the gargoyle in its mask and crown of oak leaves.

She could not smile. There was something frightening about this boy who also did not smile, but who stared at her in his dark and closed way. She walked toward him, and he moved toward her, exactly as they had in the lane, surrounded by thorns and vines and boulders that spoke.

They were only a table's distance apart when Christo caught Nicoletta's arm.

Nicoletta could not have been more astonished if an army had stopped her. She had thought her coming together with Jethro was inevitable, was destined, was a part of the history of the world before it had even happened. And yet Christo, who touched anything and whose touch meant nothing, had stopped it from happening.

"I'm over here, Nickie," Christo said eagerly. "You didn't see me."

She looked up at Christo.

She looked back at Jethro.

Jethro had already turned. There was no face at all, let alone the smile she wanted.

There was only a back. A man's broad back, unbent, uncaring. Departing.

Jethro! her heart cried after him.

But this time she did not follow him. She sat with Christo, and within moments everybody that Christo and Nicoletta knew had learned that Christo had arranged his first date ever. With Nicoletta.

The attention was better even than Madrigals. Better even than solos or applause.

And she didn't want it.

She wanted Jethro.

Chapter 5

After lunch, Jethro did not come to Art Appreciation.

Nicoletta stared, stunned, at his vacant seat.

"Is Jethro absent?" asked the teacher.

"He was here at lunch," said Nicoletta. Her lips were numb.

"He's cutting," said Mr. Marisson disapprovingly. He pressed down hard with his pencil in the attendance book.

He cut class because I cut him, thought Nicoletta. Oh Jethro! I was going to explain it to you — I was going to —

But what was there to explain? She had behaved terribly. She had arranged to meet Jethro in the cafeteria. He had done so and then what had she done? Walked off with another boy.

His empty seat mesmerized her as much as the occupied seat had.

His name filled her head and her heart, as if it really were her heartbeat: *Jeth-ro. Jeth-ro.*

Like a nursery rhyme her head screamed Jeth-ro, Jeth-ro. And of course, after school up came Chris-to, Chris-to, smiling and eager and offering her a ride home.

It was by car that romance was established. When a boy gave you rides, or you gave him rides, it meant either you lived next door and had no choice, or you were seeing each other. If you didn't want the school to make that interpretation, you had to fill your car with extras. Christo had always filled his van with extras. But now he stood alone. He must have told them already that they had to find another way home. For the usual van crowd was not there and the much-complimented Anne-Louise was not in evidence.

But Nicoletta could not go home with Christo.

She had to find Jethro. She had to go back down that lane, follow that shortcut he took to his house, and locate him.

How many lies it took to make Christo go on without her! How awful each one of them was. Because, of course, he had to believe her lies, or else know that she was dumping him. Know that she did not want to be alone with him and go for a ride with him.

When you're in love, the possibility that the object of your love has better things to do is the worst of all scenes.

So Christo just smiled uncertainly and said at last, "I'll call you tonight."

"Great," said Nicoletta, smiling, as if it were great.

They did not touch. For Christo it was the not-touching of a crush; physical desire so intense it pulled him back instead of rushing him on. For Nicoletta, it was a heart that lay elsewhere.

But Christo did not know.

Love rarely does.

Nicoletta waited inside the lobby until she saw Christo's van disappear.

And then she gathered her books and her belongings and ran out the school doors, up the road, across the street, and down the quiet lane.

There was no Jethro ahead of her. Of course not. He had left at noon, abandoning his lunch and his classes. Because of her.

She ran, and was quickly out of breath.

Today there was no sun. The last of the snow had vanished into the brown earth. The words Jamie had used were now, horribly, the right ones. These woods were dank and dark.

At the end of the lane she saw the boulder,

big and scarred and motionless. Of course it's motionless, she said to herself, it's a rock. They're always motionless.

And yet the huge stone sat there as if it had just returned from some dreadful errand.

The stone waited for her.

It's a rock, she said to herself. Put there by a glacier. That's all it is.

She might have come to the end of the world instead of the end of a little dirt road. The sky lay like an unfriendly blanket over a woods that was silent as tombs.

She clung to her books as if to a shield. As if spears might come from behind that great gray stone and pierce her body. It took all her courage to edge around the boulder.

On the other side of the rock was a footpath of remarkable straightness. In a part of the world that was all ups and downs, crevices and hills, rocky cliffs and hidden dells, here was an utterly flat stretch of land and a trail from a geometry test: The quickest way between two points is a straight line.

What are the two points? thought Nicoletta. Is his house at the other end?

Jethro, she thought. I'm coming. Where are you? What will I say to you when I find you? Why am I looking?

She walked down the trail.

When she looked back over her shoulder, the boulder was watching her.

She whimpered, and picked up speed, running again, trying to turn a corner, so the stone could not see her. But there were no corners and no matter how far she ran, the stone was still there.

The silence was complete.

She could hear nothing of the twentieth century. No motors, no turnpikes. No doors slamming, no engines revving, no planes soaring.

The only sounds were her own sounds, trespassing in this dark and ugly place.

Abruptly the trail descended. She heaved a sigh of relief as mounded earth blocked her from the terrible boulder. She wondered where she would come out, and if perhaps she could return to her own home from another direction. She did not want to go back on that path.

The trees ended, and the vines ceased crawling.

The ground was clear now, and the path became a narrow trail on top of a man-made earthen embankment. Suddenly there were lakes on each side of her, deep, black, soundless lakes with a thin, crackled layer of ice. She could go neither left nor right. Not once had there been a choice, a turning place, a fork in the road. Now she could not even blunder off into the meadow or the forest, because the trail was the only place to put a foot.

The trail ended.

She could not believe it.

It had stopped. Stopped dead. It simply did not go on.

In front of her was a rock face, a hundred feet high. Behind her lay the narrow path and the twin lakes.

She was being watched. She could feel eyes everywhere, assessing her, wondering what she would do next. They were not friendly eyes.

She wanted to scream Jethro's name, but even drawing a breath seemed like a hostile act in this isolated corner. What would a shout do? What horrible creatures would appear if she screamed?

She put a hand out so she could rest against the rock face, and her hand went right through the rock.

She yanked her hand back to the safety of her schoolbook clasp. Tears of terror wet her cheeks. Mommy, she thought. Daddy. Jamie. I want to go home. I don't want to be here.

It was a cave.

It was so black, so narrowly cut into the cliff, that at first she had not seen it. It was nothing natural. It had been chipped by some ancient tool. The opening was a perfect rectangle. She did not even have to duck her head walking in.

The wonder was that she did walk in.

Even as she was doing it, she was astonished at herself. She — a girl who hated the dark, or being alone in the dark, or even thinking of the dark — was voluntarily entering an unknown cave. Was she so terrorized that terror had become an anesthetic, flattening her thoughts? Or was she finally getting a grip on her ridiculous, fabricated fears and handling them like an adult?

She stepped into the cave.

She had expected absolute black darkness, especially with her own body blocking whatever weak sunlight might penetrate at this angle, but the cave walls themselves seemed to emanate light. They were smooth and polished like marble. She slid a bare hand over them and the texture was rich and satisfying. The cave was not damp or batlike. It seemed more like an entrance to a magnificent home, where she would find beautiful tapestries and perhaps a unicorn.

She followed a shaft of light. Even when the cave turned and the opening to the world behind her disappeared. Even when the cave went down and she had to touch the wall for support.

Part of her knew better.

Part of her was screaming, *Stop this! Get out! Go home! Think!*

But more of her was drawn on, as all humans are drawn to danger: the wild and impossible excitement of the unknown and the unthinkable.

She did not know how far she went into the cave. She did not know how many minutes she spent moving in, deeper in, farther from the only opening she knew.

She paused for breath, and in that moment the cave changed personality. Gone was the elegant marble. In a fraction of a second, the walls had turned to dripping horrors.

Holes and gaping openings loomed like death traps.

Whistling sounds and flying creatures filled her ears and her hair.

She whirled to run out, but the cave went dark.

Completely, entirely dark.

Her scream filled the cave, echoing off the many walls, pouring out the holes like some burning torch.

"Jethro!" she screamed. "Jethro!"

She touched a wall and it was wet with slime. She fell to her knees, scraping them on something, and then . . . the something moved beneath her.

She was not falling. The earth was lifting, arranging itself against her, attaching itself to her. She actually tried to fall. Anything to free herself from the surface of the underworld that clung to her, sucking like the legs of starfish.

"Jethro!" she screamed again.

Tentacles of slime and dripping stone wrapped themselves around her body.

I will die here. Nobody will know. Who could ever find me here? Nobody has been in this cave in a hundred years. This is some leftover mine from olden days. Abandoned. Forgotten.

And Jethro — he could live anywhere. What on earth had made her think that the walk through the woods necessarily led to Jethro's house? What on earth had made her think that she would find Jethro by following a path that led only to a cave?

Nothing on earth, she thought. Something in hell. This is an opening to some other, terrible world.

The creatures of that other world were surfacing, and surrounding her, dragging her down with them.

"Jethro!" she screamed again, knowing that there were no creatures, there was only a mine shaft; she must stay calm, she must find her own way out. She must stop fantasizing. She must be capable.

She tried to remember the calming techniques that Ms. Quincy used before Madrigal concerts. Breathe deeply over four counts. Shake your fingertips. Roll your head gently in circles.

It turned out that you had to be pretty calm to start with in order to attempt calming techniques. Screams continued to pour from her mouth, as if somebody else occupied her.

I'm the only one here, Nicoletta told herself. I must stop screaming. This is how people die in the wilderness. They panic. I must not panic. I am the only one here and —

She was wrong.

She was not the only one there.

The cave filled with movement and smell and she was picked up, actually held in the air, by whatever else was in the cave with her.

A creature from that other, lower, darker, world.

Its skin rasped against hers like saw grass. Its stink was unbreathable. Its hair was dead leaves, crisping against each other and breaking off in her face. Warts of sand covered it, and the sand actually came off on her, as if the creature were half made out of the cave itself.

She could not see any of the thing, only feel and smell it.

It was holding her, as if in an embrace.

Would it consume her? Did it have a mouth and jaws?

Would it carry her down to wherever it lay?

Would it line its nest with her, or feed her to its young?

She was no longer screaming. Its terrible stench took too much from her lungs; she could not find the breath to scream, only to gag.

And then it carried her up — not down.

Out — not in.

And spoke.

English.

Human English.

"Never come back," it said, its voice as deep and dark as the cave itself.

She actually laughed, hysteria crawling out of her as the screams had moments before. "I won't," she said. I'm having a conversation with a monster, she thought.

"It isn't safe," it said.

"I could tell."

The walls became smooth and they glowed. The beautiful patterns of the shiny entrance surrounded them.

She looked at what held her and screamed again in horror. She had never had such a nightmare, never been caught in such a hideously vivid dream. The features of the thing were humanoid, but the flesh dripped, like cave walls.

Old sayings came true: There was literally light at the end of the tunnel.

Real light. Sunlight. Daylight!

She flung herself free of the thing's terrible embrace. Falling, slipping, running all at the same instant, Nicoletta got out of the cave.

Never had a gray sky been so lovely, so free, so perfect.

Never had dark lakes and bleak woods been so appealing, so friendly.

She held up her hands to the real world, incredibly grateful to be back. The sight of her bare hands reminded her she no longer held her schoolbooks.

The thing stood slightly behind the mouth of the cave, so that its shadow but not itself was visible. The books sat neatly in a pile by the opening. Had Nicoletta set them down like that?

"Don't come back," the thing said again, with a sadness so terrible that Nicoletta dissolved from fear into pity. Nicoletta knew what loneliness was, and she heard it in that awful voice.

It lives down there, she thought. It's caught forever in that terrible dark.

How ridiculously petty to be fretting for a larger house and a separate room. She could be sentenced to *this*, whatever this was! She would never have gotten out without this creature's help. She would have died down there.

She felt a strange bond between them, the bond of rescuer and rescued. Her need to run and scream had ended with the sunlight. "Are you alone?" she asked.

"No," it said sadly. "Alone would be better."

What terrible company it must have, to think alone was better.

"Don't come back," it whispered. "Not ever. Don't even think about it. Not ever. *Promise*. Promise me that you will never even think about coming back here."

Chapter 6

A strange and difficult promise. *Don't even think about it.*

A promise not to go back would be easy to keep. Neither wild horses nor nuclear bombs could have made Nicoletta go back.

But not even *think* about it?

Not wonder who or what it was? What sort of life it led?

Not wonder about its name, or gender, or species?

It had saved her life. Who could forget such an event?

A strange evening followed that weird and inexplicable afternoon.

She walked through a house which only that morning she had hated. But how wonderful it was! For it had walls and warmth, lamps and pillows. It had love and parents and food and music.

Her sister did not infuriate her. Jamie actually seemed beautiful and even worthy. She was alive and giggling and pesky, which was how little sisters are meant to be. What did Jamie have to do with caves and monsters?

Nicoletta had always told her family everything. Other girls who said they could not communicate with their families confused Nicoletta. What could they mean? Nicoletta simply arrived home from school and started talking. So did Jamie. So did Mother and Dad. Not communicate?

For the first time in her life, she did not communicate.

She did not tell them about the quiet lane, the staring stone, the straight path, the descending cave. As for the creature who brought her up from the depths, by the time she had reached home, she could no longer believe in him herself. He could have been nothing but an hallucination. She had not known her imagination was so active; in fact, Nicoletta thought of herself as having little or no imagination.

Such a thing could not have happened, and therefore it had not happened.

And so she remained silent, and shared none

of it, and it swelled in her mind, filling her with confusion and disbelief.

Several times she drew a deep breath to begin the story somewhere. Each time she looked away and said nothing. She did not want a lecture on safety. Safety alone could consume weeks of scolding. Just the idea of Nicoletta walking alone into an unknown woods would outrage her parents. But when she told them she walked straight into an abandoned mine shaft — well, please.

But what kind of mine could it have been? Who had mined it? Who had smoothed those lovely walls, and what mineral caused the elegant glow?

A monster lives in it, she imagined herself saying to her father. The monster has cave skin: sand skin: rock skin. It has calcified leaves for hair and crumbling stones for fingers.

It occurred to Nicoletta that her family might just laugh.

She did not want anybody laughing at the creature. It had saved her. It had carried her out.

And yet — she wanted to talk about it. She was a talker and a sharer by nature.

And more than anything, she wanted to go back.

On that very first evening, sitting quietly at

the dining table — while Jamie did geography homework and Nicoletta pretended to do algebra — while her mother balanced the checkbook and her father finished the newspaper — Nicoletta thought — *I want to go back*.

Jethro was familiar with the path. Surely he had followed it to its end at least once. Jethro would not have flinched from entering that shining cavern. He would have walked in as she had.

That's why Jethro didn't want me to follow him any farther, she thought. He's met the monster, too! The monster asked Jethro never to tell either!

In school tomorrow she would ask him about it. She would see if his eyes flickered when she said "cave." It would not be breaking a promise if you talked with a person who already knew.

When the phone rang and it was Christo, Nicoletta could hardly remember who that was. She could barely remember Madrigals, her group of friends and her great loss. Christo wanted to know what color dress she would wear. Nicoletta actually said, "Wear to what?"

Christo laughed uneasily. "The dance Friday, Nicoletta."

She detested rudeness in people. She was ashamed of herself for not having her thoughts where they belonged. Quickly she said, "I was kidding. I'm sorry. It was dumb. I have this lovely pale pink dress. Are you getting me flowers? I adore flowers."

Nobody had ever given her flowers. Why was she implying that she had had the honor often?

Christo said his mother was recommending white. Roses or carnations.

Nicoletta said she would love white roses.

But before her eyes was the blackness of caves.

And inside her mind was a slipperiness. She had a secret now, she who had never had a secret. The secret wanted to be in the front of her mind, consuming her thoughts. She had to push it to the rear, and behave like a normal human being, and flirt with Christo and miss Madrigals and study algebra.

"Let's have lunch again tomorrow," Christo said.

She hesitated. What about Jethro? Well, she would talk to Jethro in Art Appreciation. Or follow him again.

"Yes," she said. "Lunch was fun today." She couldn't even remember lunch today.

And lunch the next day blurred as well.

She had difficulty paying attention to Christo. Everything she did was a fake. She was sufficiently aware to know that, and be appalled at herself. She knew that Christo half-knew.

She knew he was thinking that perhaps this was what girls were like: that easy friendship evaporated, to be replaced by hot and cold flirtation. And she knew that while he was hurt by her distance, he was also fascinated by it. He had never experienced that with a girl; all the girls adored him. Christo was thinking more about Nicoletta than he had ever thought about a girl.

And am I flattered? thought Nicoletta. Am I falling in love with him? Am I even thinking about my first formal dance and my first bouquet?

No.

I am thinking about a boy in art whose last name I do not even know. I am thinking about a cave in which I thought I might die and a monster in whom I no longer believe because there is no such thing as a monster.

Lunch ended and she rushed to Art Appreciation, barely taking time to wave good-bye to Christo.

"He would have kissed you," whispered Rachel as the girls rushed up the stairwell together. "He wanted to kiss you in front of everybody, I can tell. I know these things."

Two days ago, Nicoletta had thought that the loss of her girlfriends in Madrigals would kill her. Now she just wanted Rachel to vanish so that she could concentrate on Jethro.

And because passing period was only three minutes, Rachel had no choice but to vanish, and Nicoletta entered Art Appreciation.

Jethro was present.

She was filled with exuberance. It was like turning into a hot-air balloon. Flames of delight lifted her heart and soul.

"Jethro," she said.

His body stiffened in his seat but he did not turn.

She knelt beside his chair and looked up into his face.

He remained frozen. How perfect he was. Like a statue — sculpture from some Dark Age. She wanted to stroke his face and hair, as if he were artwork himself, and she could study the curves and surfaces.

He relented and looked down at her.

"I'm sorry about lunch," she said, keeping her voice so soft that nobody could share their words. "But I have to talk to you. Something happened yesterday, Jethro. I have to tell you about it."

She stared into his eyes, looking for a clue to his thoughts.

Jethro wet his lips, as if she were frightening him.

"After school?" she said. "Let's walk down the lane together."

He was shocked.

She might have suggested that they bomb a building.

"Just a walk," she whispered. "Just a talk. Please."

He shivered very slightly.

She could not imagine what his thoughts were. His eyes gave her no more clues than a sculpture would give and he used no words.

The teacher cleared his throat. "Uh — Nicoletta? Excuse me?"

She got to her feet, and in the moment before she slid into her seat she stroked the back of Jethro's hand.

He spent the entire class period looking at his hand.

As if nobody had ever touched him before.

Chapter 7

They stood where they had stood before, beside the stone. With Jethro beside her, she was not afraid of the stone. It still seemed alive, as if left over from another world, it held a spirit. A woodland power. But it no longer threatened her.

"And you promised?" said Jethro.

How measured his speech was. How carefully he pondered each word before he actually put it in his mouth and used it. Nicoletta realized that everybody else she knew used speech cheaply: It meant little. To Jethro, every syllable was precious. He squandered nothing.

"I didn't actually make any promises," said Nicoletta. How she wanted to touch him again. But he was more like the stone than like a boy. He was entirely within himself, and only the few spare syllables of speech escaped his control. "I left," explained Nicoletta. "I was afraid."

Jethro nodded. "I can understand that you were afraid." His eyes looked down into an emotional cave of their own.

"I want to go back," said Nicoletta. She felt light and bright, as if she were the flame of a candle.

He was shaken. "Caves are dangerous, Nicoletta." He had never used her name before. She took his hand as if it were her possession, as if they had both agreed that she might have his hand, and again he stared at the way her fingers wrapped around his. He seemed caught in emotion so deep that there were no words for it. Perhaps even a person used to speech, like Nicoletta, could not have explained his emotion.

"Please don't go back," said Jethro. His voice was meant only for her. It was not a whisper, and yet it did not carry; it was intended to travel only as far as her ears and then stop. He sounded as if he had had a lifetime of practice at preventing his speech from being heard. It was the opposite of what anybody else did with speech. "It's dangerous, Nicoletta."

"Then you do know!" she said. "You *have* been in there, Jethro. You know what I'm talking about."

He looked at the stone and drew himself together, becoming more remote, more taut. "I know what you're talking about," he admitted.

"Let's go together," she said. She tried to pull him around the stone to the straight and silken path that lay beyond.

But he did not cooperate. "You must go home," he said. "You must not come this way again."

Nicoletta did not listen to him. She did not want warnings. She wanted Jethro. "Where do you live?" she said. "Tell me where you live!" She explored his fingers with hers, slipping between them, pressing down with her thumb, feeling his bones and sinews.

This is what falling in love is, thought Nicoletta. It's looking at a boy and wanting to know every single thing there is to know about him, and wanting to know every inch of him, and every emotion of him, and every word in him.

Jethro's eyelids trembled, closing down over his eyes as if he could shutter himself away, and then they opened wide, and he stared back into her eyes.

He loves me, too, thought Nicoletta. Still holding his hand in one of hers, she lifted her other hand to his face. As if reading mirrors, he did exactly what she did. Fingertips approached cheeks. Nicoletta and Jethro shivered with the heat of first love's first touch.

His hand slid cupped over her chin and around her face. His fingers went into her hair. He drew the gleaming yellow locks through his fingers, and wound them gently over his palm. "You have beautiful hair," he said in a husky voice. His lips pressed together, coming to a decision, while her lips opened, ready.

Kiss me, thought Nicoletta. Please kiss me. If you kiss me, it will seal this. It will be love. I can tell by the way you're standing here that you want to be in love with me. Kiss me, Jethro!

But a car came slowly, noisily, down the road.

They were jolted by the sudden sight and sound of the vehicle.

This had been a place in which the twentieth century did not come, and now it was driving right up.

She knew the car.

It was Christo's.

Jethro's breathing was ragged. "Do not tell him!" whispered Jethro with a ferocity that frightened her. "You must not tell him!" Nicoletta was stunned by the force of Jethro's command. "You have promised to keep a secret! You must keep the promise, Nicoletta!"

Christo swung out of the van, leaving the motor idling.

"*Promise*," breathed Jethro, with a terrible force, as if his lungs were going to explode.

But she did not answer him.

"Hi, Christo," she said. "Do you know Jethro?"

Christo shook his head. She introduced them, using only first names, since she did not know Jethro's last name. The young men stared at each other warily. Christo extended his right hand. They shook hands, also warily, as if they were about to be contestants in some duel.

"I'm glad you came," said Jethro. His voice calm now, even bland. "Would you mind giving Nicoletta a ride home? She shouldn't be down here. We were arguing about it. The woods are dangerous. Nobody should be in these woods without a compass."

Christo was amazed. "You don't seem like the outdoor type," he said to Nicoletta. "Do you hike? Do you camp?"

"No. Never."

"That's why I told her to stay away," said Jethro. "It's dangerous for somebody who's ignorant about it."

"I love the woods," said Christo happily. "I'll teach you, Nickie. That's what we'll do this weekend! We'll go to the state forest and hike down to the waterfalls! They're so beautiful in winter." Christo led Nicoletta to his van as he gave her a long, lyrical description of frozen waterfalls and gleaming ice.

How easily he used words! Not like Jethro, who could hardly bear to let a syllable out of his mouth. "Nice to have met you," Christo called cheerfully back to Jethro.

How strange romance is, thought Nicoletta. I was following Jethro and Christopher was following me. To Christo this is the beginning of a beautiful romance in which we share the great outdoors. I don't care about the outdoors at all. I don't care about Christo either. I care about Jethro.

And I wonder about the cave.

And the monster.

And the promise that mattered so much.

To whom was I making that promise? she thought suddenly, frowning. To the creature? Or Jethro?

Christo, backing his van down the narrow rutted lane, suddenly lifted his right hand from the wheel and stared at it. He shook his hand slightly.

"What?" said Nicoletta. Her eyes were glued to the place where Jethro had stood. He stood there no longer. He had circled the stone, and must even now be tracing the straight path. Even now Jethro was going toward the cave, on a path that seemed to go nowhere else, a path he had wanted her to promise she would never follow again.

But I will, thought Nicoletta. I will follow Jethro forever.

"There's sand on my hand," said Christo. "That guy's hand was all sandy."

Chapter 8

Never before in her life had Nicoletta intentionally done something stupid and dangerous. Her parents were cautious in all things but money. They had taught Nicoletta and Jamie to steer clear of strangers, to look both ways before crossing streets, to be home before dark. They were full of warnings and guidance, and Nicoletta had spent a lifetime listening carefully and obeying completely.

But not today.

The snow was falling lightly when she left the school building. She had hidden in the library stacks until Christopher had definitely driven away. Hidden among the dusty pages and unread texts until there was not a single soul left in the school whom she knew.

Little homework had been assigned for the night. Nicoletta was able to leave her bookbag in her locker. How strange to be unburdened, to have hands and arms free. She ran all the way, feet flying, hair streaming behind her, heart filled with excitement.

How lovely the woods were, dusted with snow, crisp and clean and pure in the fading afternoon.

The snow was dry and separate. Snowflakes touched her cheeks like kisses.

The road narrowed and she had to slow down, unable to find easy footing on the snow-hidden ruts of the dirt lane. At first she did not even see the boulder; snow had draped it like a cloak. It did not look like a stone, but like an igloo, a place that would be cozy inside. She patted the stone as she rounded it and her glove left a perfect five-fingered print.

On each side of the slim, straight path, the dry weeds stood up like snow bouquets. Ice flowers.

The snow came down more heavily.

There was no sky anymore; just a ceiling of white.

When she came to the place where pools of water lay below each side of the raised pathway, snow had covered the ice, and had Nicoletta not seen the lakes before, she would have thought they were fields; she would have thought it was safe to run over them, and dance upon them.

The cliff wall was hung with frozen water from springs deep in the earth. Snow danced in gusts, spraying against the cliff like surf and falling in drifts at the foot of the rocks.

A piece of the cliff moved toward her.

Nicoletta held out her palm like a crossing guard, as if she could stop an avalanche that way.

It was stone, and yet it walked. It was snow, and yet it bore leaves. It was a person, and yet —

It was the creature.

She could see its eyes now, living pools trapped in that terrible frame.

She could see its feet, formed not so differently from the huge icicles that hung on the cliff: things. Dripping stalagmites from the floor of the cave.

She felt no fear. The snow, falling so gently, so pure and cleanly, seemed protection. Yet snow protected nothing but ugliness. Ugliness it would hide. Filthy city alleys and rusted old cars, abandoned, broken trikes and rotting picnic tables — snow covered anything putrid and turned it to perfect sculpture.

Even the thing, the monstrous thing that had stank and dripped and scraped — it was perfect in its softly rounded snowy wrap.

"Go away," it growled. "What is the matter

with you? Don't you understand? *Go away!*"

"I want to find Jethro."

It advanced on her.

She backed up. What if I fall off the path? she thought. What if I fall down on those ponds? How thick is the ice? Will I drown here?

"Go away," it said.

"I know Jethro lives here somewhere," she said. "You must know him. He takes this path. The path stops here! Tell me where he turns off. Tell me where he goes. Tell me where to find him." She could no longer look at the thing. Its face was scaly, like a mineral, and the snow did not cling to its surface, but melted, so that it ran, like an overflowing gutter. She looked past the thing and saw the black hole of the cave. It wanted her. She could feel its eagerness to have her again. She tore her eyes away and wondered how she would get past the cave to wherever Jethro was.

"Why does he matter?" asked the thing.

Why does Jethro matter? thought Nicoletta. I don't know. Why does anybody matter? What makes you care about one person so deeply you cannot sleep?

She said, "He wasn't in school today."

The creature said nothing. It turned around and moved toward its cave.

"Don't go!" said Nicoletta. "I'm worried

about him. I like him. I want to talk to him."

It disappeared into the cavern.

Or perhaps, because it was stone and sand itself, it simply blended into, or became part of, the cliff.

She followed it. She ran right after it, inside the flat and glowing walls of the entrance.

"Stop it!" the thing bellowed. Its voice was immense, and the cave echoed with its deep, rolling voice. "Get out!"

"I love him," said Nicoletta.

In the strange silence that followed, she could see the thing's eyes. They had filled with tears.

Only humans cry. Not stones.

"Who are you?" she whispered.

But it did not answer.

The only sound was the sharp unmistakable report of a rifle. Nicoletta whirled.

"Hunters. They think I'm a bear," whispered the thing. "They'll come in here to shoot me. Poachers."

"Have they come in before?" she whispered back.

"They don't usually find the cave opening. Sometimes they see me, though, if I'm careless, and they follow me."

She could hear the loud and laughing voices of men. Cruel laughter, lusting for a kill.

72

"If they see you move, they'll shoot you," it told her. "They shoot anything that moves."

"I'll go down in the cave with you," said Nicoletta. "We'll be safe together." No snow remained on the humanoid creature. Its stink increased and its stone skin flaked away. Its hair like dead leaves snapped off and littered the floor. As long as she didn't have to touch it, or look too closely, she was not afraid of it.

"No," it said. "You must never, never, never go down in this cave."

"I did before."

"And you only got out because I brought you out. If you go any farther into the cave, the same thing will happen to you that happened to me."

"What happened to you?" she said. She forgot to whisper. She spoke out loud.

From out in the snow came a yell of satisfaction. "I see the cave!" bellowed a voice. "This way! We'll get it this time! Over here!"

The thing grabbed Nicoletta and the horrible rasp of its gruesome skin made her scream. It put its hand over her mouth and she could taste it. A swallow of disease and pollution filled her throat. She struggled against the thing but it lifted her with horrifying absolute strength. She was carried down the tunnel and into a small low-ceilinged pit beside the shaft.

"Don't make any sounds," it breathed into her ear. Its breath was a stench of rot.

She was weeping now, soaking its ghastly skin with her tears. The acid of her very own tears dissolved the thing. Its coating was soaking off onto her.

I've been such a fool, thought Nicoletta. My parents will kill me. I deserve anything I get.

She fought but the thing simply pressed her up against the back of the dark pit. When the slime of the wall came off on her cheek, Nicoletta sagged down and ceased struggling. She tried to crawl right inside herself, and just not be there in mind or in body.

But she was there. And all her senses — smell, sight, sound, touch — all of them brought her close to vomiting with horror.

If I can let the hunters know I am here, thought Nicoletta, they will save me. They'll shoot this horrible animal and take me home.

The hunters came into the cave.

There were two of them.

They had a flashlight.

She saw the light bobble past her little cavern but she knew that if they glanced in her direction, they would see only the stony side of the creature. To their eyes, the thing gripping her would look like cave wall.

She took a breath to scream but the thing's

handlike extension clapped so tightly over her mouth she could taste it, toxic and raw.

"This is neat," said one of the hunters. His voice was youthful and awestruck. "I can't imagine why I've never heard of this place. Never even seen the opening before."

"Me either," said the other one. "And I've come around here for years. Why, it's — it's — "

"It's beautiful! I'm calling the TV stations the minute we shoot that bear."

"Let's put the body right outside of the cave opening," agreed the other one. "It'll make a great camera angle."

Their voices faded. The creature's grip on Nicoletta did not.

They walked more deeply into the cave. No! she thought. They mustn't go in farther! The cave will turn! I've been at that end of it! It isn't beautiful, it's the opening to some other terrible place. I've got to warn them. I've got to stop them.

She flung herself at her captor, but its strength was many multiples of her own. Nothing occurred except bruising against its stony surface.

Her heart pounded so hard and so fast that she wondered if she would live through this.

Perhaps her own heart would kill her, giving up the struggle.

So distantly that Nicoletta was not confident of her hearing, came two long, thin cries. Human cries. Threads of despair. Cries for help.

The final shrieks before the final fall.

The two hunters, plunging down the black end of the shaft. Hitting bottom, wherever that might be.

She knew what they felt. The textures and the moving air, the shifting sands and the touching walls.

The thing released her. Her mouth and lips were free. Shock kept her silent. The entire cavern was silent.

Silence as total as darkness.

No moans from the fallen pair. No cries of pain. No shouts for help.

They had hit bottom. They were gone. Two eager young men, out for an afternoon of pleasure.

The monster's sand clung to her face and wrists. She could not move. She could not run or fight or think.

After a moment, it picked her up like a pile of coats and carried her out of the cave.

The snow was now falling so heavily that the world was obliterated.

If there was a world. Perhaps this horrible

place was the only place on earth, and it was her home.

She wept, and the tears froze on her cheeks.

"I'm sorry," it said. "I had to do that."

"How will they get out?" she said, sobbing.

"They won't."

How matter-of-factly it gave an answer. How will the hunters get out? *They won't.*

She backed away from him. "You *are* a monster," she said, and she did not mean his form, but his soul. "You let them go down in there and fall. You knew they would fall! You knew they would come to a place where there was no bottom." She began to run, slipping and falling. The path was invisible. The snow came down like a curtain between them. When she fell again, she slid periously close to the ice over the deep, black lake.

He picked her up out of the snow and set her on her feet. "I'll go with you some of the way. In this weather there will be no more of them."

He held her gloved hand and together they walked between the lakes. On the straight and slender path they could not walk abreast, and he walked ahead, clearing the snow for her.

She had given him gender and substance. Her mind had taken him out of the neuter-thing category. The monster was a he, not an it.

They reached the boulder. "Promise you

won't come back," he said. His voice was soft and sad.

Her hair prickled. Her skin shivered. Her hands inside the gloves turned to ice.

"You must go home. You must not come this way again."

She looked into the eyes. Deep, brown, human eyes. And a human voice that had said those same words to her once before.

Chapter 9

Her first real dance. Her first real date.

And Nicoletta was as uninterested as if her parents had gone and rented a movie that Nicoletta had seen twice before.

"What is the matter with you?" yelled Jamie.

True love is the matter with me, thought Nicoletta. Jethro is the matter with me. Instead of having Jethro, I'm almost the captive of Christo.

It wasn't that Christo had taken her prisoner. Christo was his usual gentlemanly self. It was more that she was not arguing about it. She was not saying no. She was allowing events with Christo to take place because they did not matter to her at all.

"I don't think you even care about Christo," said Jamie, flicking a wet towel at her half-dressed sister. "Even the middle school knows that Christo asked you out."

"They only know because you told them," said Nicoletta. "How else could they know who Christo is?"

"Nicoletta, you're so annoying. He's a football star, isn't he? Me and my friends went to every game last fall, didn't we? We won the regional championship, didn't we? He has his picture in the paper all the time, doesn't he?" Jamie made several snarling faces at her sister.

Nicoletta never thought of Christo as an athlete. She thought of him exclusively as a baritone in Madrigals. She thought of him, not in a football uniform, but in the glittering turquoise and silver he wore for concerts, a king's courtier, a royal flirt.

Christo was a football player, and she did not even know, had never attended a game, never considered his practice schedule. And Jethro. Did he play sports? What was his schedule? Where did he live?

"You don't even care what you're wearing!" complained Jamie. "You didn't even ask Mom to buy you a new dress for this!"

Her dress lay on the bed, waiting for her to put it on.

She felt as if there were a veil between her mind and her life. The veil was Jethro. She was as consumed by him as if he had set her on fire. It was difficult to see anything else. The rest of the world was out of focus, and she did not care whether she saw anything clearly but Jethro.

Jamie held the dress for her and she stepped carefully into it. It was Jamie who exclaimed over the lovely silken fabric, the way it hung so gracefully from Nicoletta's narrow waist, and dropped intoxicatingly at the neckline, like a crescent moon sweeping from shoulder to shoulder. Nicoletta had borrowed her mother's imitation ruby necklace. The racing pulse at her throat made the dark red stones beat like her own blood.

"You're in love, aren't you?" whispered Jamie suddenly.

Nicoletta turned to see herself in the long mirror.

I'm beautiful, she thought. She blinked, as if expecting the beauty not to be there at the second glance. But it was. She was truly beautiful. She had to look away. It felt like somebody else in that gown.

And it is somebody else! thought Nicoletta. It's somebody in love with Jethro, not somebody in love with Christo.

Jamie was also reflected in the mirror: a scrawny little girl, still with braces and unformed figure — a little girl utterly awestruck by her big sister. For the first time in their lives, Nicoletta was worth something to Jamie. For Nicoletta was in love, and beautiful, and going to a dance with a handsome boy.

"Do you think you'll marry Christo?" said Jamie, getting down to basics. "What's his last name? What will your name be when you get married? I'll be your maid of honor, won't I?"

But Christo's last name did not matter. Only Jethro's.

Who is he? thought Nicoletta. *Where* is he?

Love was like clean ice.

Nicoletta skated through the evening. All things were effortless, all motions were gliding, all conversations spun on her lips.

Christo was proud of her, and proud that he was with her.

And if she glittered, how was he to know she glittered for someone else?

They left the dance shortly after midnight. Snow had begun again.

There was a full moon, and each snowflake was a falling crystal. The night world was equally black and silver. Even the shadows gleamed.

They drove slowly down the quiet streets, rendered perfect by the first inch of snow.

"Where are we going?" said Nicoletta.

"That road," said Christo. He smiled at her.

"I never noticed that road before. It looked quiet."

He wants to kiss, thought Nicoletta. He is going to drive me down Jethro's road, to park at the end of the lane where Jethro's stone will see us. What if the stone tells? I know they talk. I don't want Jethro to find out about Christo.

She was dizzy with the magic of her thoughts. There is no stone, she told herself, and if there is one, nobody talks to it.

Jethro had not been in school. The gloomy skies and early dark of winter had been a perfect reflection of Nicoletta's emptiness when there was no Jethro in Art Appreciation. He was the only art she appreciated.

How she wanted Jethro to see her in this gown!

For she was beautiful. She had been the princess of every girl's dream at that dance. She had been as lovely as if spun from gold, as delicate as lace, as perfect as love.

She saw herself in the snowy night, floating down the path, her long gown flowing behind her, her golden hair glittering with diamonds of snow. She saw herself untouched by cold or by fear, dancing through the dark like a princess in a fairy tale to find her prince.

O Jethro! she thought. Where are you? What

are you thinking? Why weren't you in school? Are you ill? Are you afraid of me? What promises do you have to keep? What does the stone know about you that I do not?

Driving with his left hand, Christopher touched her bare shoulder with his right. He was hot and dry, burned by the fever of wanting Nicoletta.

She thought only of Jethro, and of Jethro's hand. The first time he touched Nicoletta, his fingers had not felt human. The first time he touched Christo, he had left behind grains of sand.

A strange and terrible thought had formed in Nicoletta's mind, but she refused to allow it a definite shape.

Christopher kissed her once, and then again. The third time he shuddered slightly, wanting a hundred times more than this — wanting no car, no time limit, no clothing in the way. The calm young man who easily flirted with or touched any girl because it meant nothing, was not the one driving the van tonight.

Touching meant a great deal to Christo tonight.

Think of Christo, Nicoletta told herself, accepting the kisses but not kissing back. But she could not think of him at all. She could hardly see him. He felt evaporated and diffuse. She felt sleazy and duplicitous. What have I done? thought Nicoletta. What have I let happen? How am I going to get out of this? "Good night, Christo," she said courteously. "And thank you. I had a lovely time."

She put her hand on the door handle.

Christo stared at her. "Nickie, we're in the woods, not your driveway."

But she was out of the van, standing in her fragile, silver dancing slippers on the crust of the snow. She knew she would not break through, she would not get snow in these shoes. She touched the ruby necklace. The moon came out from behind the snow-laden clouds, and rested on her face and her throat. The ruby and the red rose of her cheeks were the only heat in the forest.

Like a silver creature of the woods, she found the path, swirling and laughing to herself.

"Nickie?" said Christo. He was out of the van, he was following her. He could not stay on the surface of the crusted snow, as she could. His big feet and strong legs slogged where she had danced. "You don't even have a coat!" he cried.

The boulder carried a shroud of snow. Nicoletta was a candle flickering in the dark. She quickstepped around the immense rock. The boulder shrugged its shoulders as Christo passed and dropped its load of snow upon him. Muffled under layers of white, his cry to Nicoletta did not reach her ears. "Wait up!" he said to her. "Don't do this, Nickie. Nickie, what are you doing?"

She was in a dance choreographed by an unknown, moonlit hand. She had a partner, unseen and unknown, and the only thing was to keep up, to stay with the rhythm, her skirts making scallop shells around her bare stockinged legs, her feet barely touching the white snow, her hands in synchrony, touching, holding, waving.

Christo struggled free from the snow and circled the boulder.

He could see her, her gown luminous as the stars, her hair like golden music. He could not imagine what she was doing, but he did not care. She was too lovely and the evening was too extraordinary for reason. He simply wanted to catch up, to be with her, to see her eyes as she danced this unearthly dance.

When he caught up to her, she was dancing on a balance beam between two black-iced ponds. The path was so narrow his heart stopped. What if she fell? What could she be thinking of? He was too out of breath to shout her name again, he whose breath control and athletic strength were his strong assets. The stillness of the night was so complete it was like crystal, a call from him would shatter the glass in which they danced.

A black, black hole at the end of Nicoletta's narrow danger opened wide, and opened wider.

Christo stared, fascinated, unable to think at all, unable to shout warnings if warnings were needed.

From the side of the ice-dripping, rock walked rock. Moving rock. The rock and Nicoletta danced together for a moment while Christo tried to free himself from ribbons of confusion. What is going on? he thought.

It was possible that the night had ended and he was deep in a dream, one of those electrical-storm dreams, in which vivid pictures leap and toss like lightning in a frightened sky.

"Nicoletta?" he said at last.

She spun, as if seeing him for the first time, and the rock spun with her, and it had a face.

The rock was a person.

Chapter 10

"You brought him here," it said to her.

She knew who he was now, but not why or how. She wanted to talk to him. Not just this night, but every night and forever. She wanted him to be the only person she ever talked to.

But he was not a person. He was a thing.

"When do you change?" she said to him. "When are you one of us?"

"I am always one of you," he said desperately. "How could you have brought Christo? How could you betray me?"

"I would never betray you. I love you."

He released her, and the rough granite of him scraped her painfully. There was more red now under the moon: her rubies, her cheeks, and her one drop of blood.

"Go!" he breathed. "Go. Convince him I am not."

Convince him I am not.

Not what? Not who?

She was alone now between the lakes and Christo was trying to join her, his large feet clumsy on the tilting ice and snow. "I'm coming, Christo!" she said, and ran toward him, but she was clumsy now, too. Her partner of the silence and snow was gone; her choreography failed her.

She slipped first, and Christo slipped second.

They were a yard apart, too far to touch, too far to catch.

At first she was not afraid, because she knew that even falling through the ice, the creature would save her, lift her, carry her out.

But the sharp tiny heel of her silver shoe punctured the ice at the same moment that Christo's big black shoe cracked it, and as the frigid water crept up her stockings, she realized that the creature would not save her, any more than it had saved the hunters. What mattered most to it was being unknown, and being untouched, and being safe itself.

Christo and I will drown, she thought. We will fall as far beneath the black water as the hunters fell in the black shaft. We will die in ice and evil cold.

She thrashed desperately, but that only made the hole in the ice larger.

Christo said, in a normal high school boy's

voice, "I can't believe I have done anything as stupid as this. Don't tell anybody, that's all I ask." He was crouching at the water's edge, having pulled himself back. He grabbed her hand and waist and yanked her unceremoniously to dry land. "Let's get out of here before we get frostbite." He hustled her along the straight path and back into the woods and back around the boulder.

Nicoletta was afraid the boulder would roll upon them, would crush their wet feet beneath its glacial tons, but it ignored them. Back in the van, Christo turned on the motor and then immediately the heat, with the blower on high.

After a moment he looked at her, reassessing what had happened and who she was.

He knows now, thought Nicoletta. He knows who I love and where I go and what matters most.

But he did not know. People in love seldom do.

"You," said Christo finally, "are not what I expected." He was laughing. He was thrilled. Nicoletta had proved to be full of well-kept secrets, a girl whose hobbies were not the usual, and he was even more proud of being with her than he had been at the dance.

Christo started to list the things they would do together — things he probably thought were unusual and exciting. To Nicoletta they sounded impossibly dull. They were of this world. They were commonplace.

Nicoletta had a true love now, from another world, a world without explanation or meaning, and she did not care about Christo's calendar.

The light was on in the bedroom Nicoletta shared with Jamie when Christo pulled into the Storms's driveway. Jamie had definitely not gone to bed. Her little face instantly appeared, and she shaded the glass with her two hands so that she could see into the dark.

Christo grinned. "We have to give your little sister a show for her money," he said.

No! thought Nicoletta, shrinking. I can't kiss you now. I'm in love with another — another what?

Man? Boy? Rock? Thing? Beast?

Or was she in love with a murderer?

She thought of the two men falling to the depths of the cave.

Where are we going? they would have said to each other.

Down.

Down forever, down to certain death.

He could have prevented the hunters from dying, she thought.

Then she thought, No, he couldn't. They

would have killed him first, shot him, it was self-defense, in a way.

Her thoughts leapt back and forth like a tennis ball over a net.

It came to her, as black and bleak as the lakes in the dark, that she had forgotten those two men. They had fallen out the bottom of her mind just as they fell out the bottom of the cave.

Love is amoral, she thought. Love thinks only of itself, or of The Other.

There is no room in love for passersby.

Those hunters. They had passed by, all right.

Did they have wives? Children? Mothers? Jobs?

Nobody will ever find them, thought Nicoletta. They will never be buried. They will never come home. Nobody will ever know.

Unless I tell.

"Good night," said Christo softly. He walked her up the steps, dizzy with love. Together they stared at the blank wooden face of the door, at the bare nail where last December a Christmas wreath had hung.

Christo's kiss was long and deep and intense. His lips contained enough energy to win football games, to sing entire concerts. When he finally stopped, and tried to find enough breath to speak, he couldn't, and just went back to the car.

Behind Nicoletta the door was jerked open and she fell inside, her heart leaping with memories of caves and black lakes, of dancing in front of rock faces that opened like the jaws of mountain spirits.

"Ooooooh, that was so terrific!" squealed Jamie, flinging her arms around her sister. "He really kissed you! Wow, what a kiss! I was watching through the peephole. Oooooooh, I can't wait to tell my friends."

Nobody could ever accuse a little sister of good timing.

"Get lost, Jamie."

"Forget it. We share a bedroom. I'll never be lost. Tell me everything or I'll never let you sleep. I'll borrow all your clothes. I'll get a parakeet and keep the cage over your bed. I'll spill pancake syrup in your hair."

"Go for it," said Nicoletta. She walked past her pesky sister and into the only room in the teeny house where you were allowed to shut the door and be alone. In the bathroom mirror she stared at herself.

Mirror, mirror, on the wall, who is the fairest of them all?

There were answers behind the silvered

glass. If she could only look in deeply enough, she would know.

I didn't look deeply enough into the cave either, she thought.

I have to go back.

Further down.

Deeper in.

Chapter 11

"Daddy and I are going to see the Burgesses today," said Mother. "This is the first free Saturday we've had in so long!"

Mr. Burgess was Daddy's old college roommate. It was a long drive and when Mother and Daddy went to see Sally and Ralph, they stayed all afternoon and sometimes long into the night.

Yes! thought Nicoletta. I'll have the time to scout out the cave. Nicoletta tightened her bathrobe around her and thought of the long, unsupervised day ahead and what yummy food she would eat to sustain herself. Doughnuts, she thought, Gummi bears, ice cream, chocolate chips out of the bag, and barbecue potato chips. She would take some to Jethro. She would wear a backpack filled with junk food, and —

"Nicoletta," said her mother, in her high,

firm, order-giving voice, "you'll stay home and baby-sit for Jamie."

"Baby-sit for Jamie?" Nicoletta repeated incredulously. She needed to get out there in the snow and find Jethro! And they were making her stay home and baby-sit her stupid sister who was perfectly capable of taking care of herself?

Nicoletta tipped way backward in her wooden breakfast table chair, rolling her eyes even farther backward, to demonstrate her total disgust.

Luckily Jamie felt the same way. "Baby-sit?" she shrieked. "Mother! I am eleven years old. I do not need a sitter and I am not a baby. Furthermore, if I did need one, I would want one more capable, more interesting, and more worth your money than Nickie."

It was agreed that the girls could take care of themselves separately, as long as they promised not to fight, not to argue, and not to do anything foolish.

"I promise," said Nicoletta, who had never meant anything less.

"I promise," said Jamie, who lived for fights and arguments and would certainly start both, the minute their parents were out of sight.

Their car backed out of the driveway, leaving deep lacelike treads in the snow. The sky was a thin, helpless blue, as if its own veins had chilled and even the sky could no longer get warm.

But Jamie did not start a fight.

"Make pancake men," she said pleadingly to her sister. This was one of the few episodes out of the *Little House* series that Jamie considered worthy. Nicoletta was excellent at it, too. Nobody could pour pancake batter like Nicoletta.

So Nicoletta made pancake men and then struggled with pancake women, although skirts were harder to pour. They ate by cutting away limbs with the sides of their forks: having first the arms, then the legs.

Jamie drowned some of her men in syrup, pouring it on until their little pancake heads were under water, so to speak.

There was nothing quite so filling as pancakes. When you had had pancakes for breakfast, you were set for a hard day's work. Nicoletta dressed, carefully hiding her excitement from Jamie. Jamie loved Saturday morning cartoons and with luck would not even hear the door close as Nicoletta slipped out. With extremely good luck, she would still be cartooning and junk-fooding when Nicoletta returned in the afternoon.

There had been enough money last year for

Nicoletta to purchase a wonderful winter wardrobe. She wanted to be seen against the snow. A scarlet ski jacket with silver trim zipped tightly against the cold. Charcoal-gray pants tucked into white boots with furry linings. She wore no hat. The last thing she wanted to do was cover her hair.

She loosened it from its elastics and let it flow free, the only gold in a day of silver and white.

"Where are you going?" yelled Jamie, hearing the door open after all.

"Out." Nicoletta liked the single syllable. The strength of it pleased her. The total lack of information that it gave, increased the sense of secrecy and plotting. She stood for a moment in the doorway, planning her strategy. She'd be warm inside her puffy jacket, but the pants were not enough and the boots were more for show than snow. She needed earmuffs in the fierce wind, but would die before wearing them.

"Nicoletta!" screamed her sister, who never called her that. The scream soared upward with rising fear. "Nicoletta!" Loud. Louder than it should be for anything less than blood. "Nicoletta, come here!"

She flew through the house, remembering emergency numbers, fighting for self-control, reminding herself to stay calm. Was Jamie bleeding? Was Jamie —

Jamie was fine. Curled in a ball on the easy chair, with Mother's immense purple velour bathrobe draped around her like Cinderella's gown.

"This better be good," said Nicoletta. "Talk fast before I kill you."

"Kill me for what?" said Jamie.

"Frightening me."

Jamie was gratified to have frightened Nicoletta. Nicoletta could think only of time lost, time she needed to find and talk to Jethro. Time in the winter woods, time behind the swollen boulder. Get to the point! she thought, furious in the wake of her unreasoning fear.

Jamie pointed to the local news channel.

"You called me in here to look at something on TV?" shouted Nicoletta.

"Shut up and listen."

A distraught woman was sobbing. "My husband! My husband Rob!" she said. "We don't know what happened to him! He never came home last night. Or Al either. They must be hurt." The woman's shoulders heaved with weeping. "I don't know," she whispered. "They're lying out there in the snow. I know they are. Too weak to call for help. Or maybe they fell through unsafe ice. I don't know. But Rob didn't come home."

As if she, too, had fallen through unsafe ice, Nicoletta grew colder and colder, sinking to the depths of her soul.

"See," said Jamie, "what happened is, these two hunters went out yesterday morning and they never came home. Isn't that creepy? They took a day off from work to go hunting *and they never came home.*"

I forgot them, she thought. I forgot them right away. I yelled at the monster once and then I forgot again. But those were people. Real people.

"What if she never finds out?" said Jamie in a low, melodramatic voice. "You missed it, Nick, but they showed her little kids. The kids are too little to know what's going on. They just held hands and stared at the camera. You know, that goopy, gaping look little kids have."

Children, thought Nicoletta. I went back and danced on the snow while little children waited for a daddy who is not coming home. And I knew, I knew all along.

Something in her congealed. She felt more solid, but not flesh and blood solid. Metallic. As if she were no longer human, but more of a robot, built of wires and connections in a factory.

Because I didn't react like a human, she

thought. A human would have gone to the police, called an ambulance, taken rescue teams to the cave to bring the hunters up. And what did I do? I obeyed a voice telling me to keep its secrets.

The reporter's face became long and serious. "In this temperature," she said grimly, "in this weather, considering tonight's forecast, there is little hope that the men will survive, if indeed they are alive at this moment. They must be found today."

Nicoletta's stomach tried to throw up the pancake men.

She forced herself to be calm. She supervised every inside and outside muscle of herself. It seemed even more robotic. And it worked. She knew from Jamie's glance that her body and face revealed nothing.

"Search teams are combing the areas where the men are thought to have been," said the reporter. "We will return with updates." The long, grim face vanished into a perky smile, as if the reporter, too, were a robot programmed for certain expressions. "Now," she said cheerily, "back to your regular programming!"

Jamie, who always preferred regular programming, and never wanted interruptions, sighed happily and tucked herself more deeply into her mother's robe.

Nicoletta backed out of the room. She stared down at the bright, sparkling outfit she had chosen to shine in the snowy woods, so Jethro would see her.

I know where they are . . . but if I tell . . . his secret . . . my promise . . .

Anyway, they're dead. It isn't as if anybody could rescue them now. They have a grave, too — farther underground than an undertaker would put them.

It was not funny. Not funny at all. And yet a snickery laugh came out of her mouth and hung in the air like frost. She had to pull her mouth back into shape with both hands.

What shall I do? Does a promise to a monster count when wives are sobbing and children have lost their father? Of course not.

But in her heart, she knew there had been no promise to a monster. The promise had been to . . .

But even now she could not finish the sentence. It was not possible and she was calm enough to know that much.

But it was true, and she had seen enough to know that as well.

First, I'll find him, she told herself. We'll talk. I'll explain to him that I have to notify authorities. Then —

A small, bright yellow car whipped around

the corner, slipping dangerously on the ice, and zooming forward to slip again as it rushed up her driveway. Rachel, who aimed for every ice patch and shrieked with laughter at every skid. Rachel, coming for a Saturday morning gossip.

Nicoletta could not believe this was happening to her. First she had to make breakfast with her sister. Now she had to waste time with her best friend.

Rachel leapt out of the driver's side and Cathy from the passenger side. It wasn't enough that she would be saddled with one friend; now there were two. They slammed their doors hard enough to rock the little car and purposely leapt onto untouched snow, rather than using the path, tagging each other and giggling.

She was framed in the doorway anyhow; there was no escape; so she flung it open and said hi.

"Nickie!" they cried. "You have to tell us everything. We're dying to hear about it."

Her heart tightened. *How could Rachel and Cath know?* She had said nothing! Only Christo had been there, and he'd had no sense of what was going on. He'd been too in love with Nicoletta to see anything.

And yet Rachel and Cathy knew.

Nicoletta struggled to remain composed.

She could not talk to anybody until she had talked to Jethro. That was all, that was that.

Rachel flung her arms around Nicoletta. "It's terrible not to see you all the time," she said. "We're so out of touch. Now get inside where it's toasty-oasty warm and tell us all about it." Rachel shoved Nicoletta into her own house.

Cathy tap-danced after them. "You're so lucky, Nickie," she said, admiring her own steps. "Did you dance all night?"

They even knew that she had danced under the moon and across the snow!

"Hi, Jamie," said Rachel. "Are you still worthless or have you improved since we saw you last?"

"I'm flawless," said Jamie. "Get out of my living room. I'm watching television. But if you pay me, I'll describe Christo's good-night kiss. It was very long and — "

Christo.

This was about Christo! The dance at Top o' the Town. Not the dance to find Jethro.

Nicoletta surfaced. It was sticky coming up, as if, like the pancake men, she had drowned under syrup.

How quickly can I get rid of them? she wondered. She would have to give them every detail, assuming she could remember any details; and then what excuse could she use to make them leave her alone? She wondered if there was any way she could get Rachel to drive her to the dead-end road, save her that long hike. She could think of no way to explain being dropped off there.

"And then," said Jamie, accepting a pack of Starburst candy in payment, "Christo staggered back to the car like a drunk. Except he was drunk with Nickie." Jamie laughed insanely. "Men," she said, shaking her head in dismay. Clearly she had expected men to have higher standards in love than her own sister.

"Oh, that's beautiful," sighed Cathy. "Come on, Nickie, into your room for your version. We've already had Christo's and now Jamie's."

"You've already had Christo's?"

"Of course. We had an extra rehearsal this morning. At Anne-Louise's. She has the most wonderful house, Nickie. It's on Fairest Lane, as a matter-of-fact. Her family bought the house three down from your old one, and her living room is huge. The whole chorus can fit in easily. Plus she has a grand piano, not to mention a fabulous electric keyboard. There's nothing that keyboard isn't programmed to do."

"Cathy," muttered Rachel. "I don't think Nickie is thrilled to hear that."

Cathy apologized desperately.

"It doesn't matter," said Nicoletta. It didn't. All that mattered was getting to the boulder, the path, the two lakes, the cave.

And Jethro.

Is he the monster? she thought. How can he be? How can anybody be?

"So," said Rachel, hugging herself with eagerness. She lowered her voice. Excitedly she whispered, "Are you in love with him?"

Nicoletta stared into the faces of her former friends. Still friends, she supposed. Friends because they had not forgotten her . . . and yet, friends she'd forgotten.

Am I in love with him? she thought. Which him do we mean?

She told them many lies. At the time she uttered each sentence, she swore to remember it, so they wouldn't know she was lying, but she tripped continually. She could not remember one lie even through the following lie.

Cathy and Rachel thought it was wonderful. "You're so dizzy with love, you can't even keep your first date straight," accused Rachel. She hugged Nicoletta, cementing something, but Nicoletta did not know what.

"I'm jealous," added Cathy.

The doorbell rang.

"Get it! yelled Jamie. "I'm busy."

Nicoletta went to the door. In this tiny

house, everybody was adjacent to everything and everyone.

It was Christo.

No, she thought. No, not now. I've told enough lies. I can't tell more.

Just seeing her brought a laugh to Christo's lips. "Hi, Nicoletta," he said, trembling over these simple words. It was not a tremble of nervousness, but of sheer pleasure to see her. But of course, it was not only Nicoletta he saw. With a touch of disappointment, he added, "Hi, Cathy. Hi, Rachel."

"We're just leaving," said the girls, nudging each other, pushing the romance along.

Don't leave me alone with Christo! How will I ever get to Jethro if Christo is here? I don't mind lying to you two. If I could explain everything to you, you wouldn't mind. But Christo! He would mind.

For there is no explanation for loving somebody else.

Chapter 12

"Let's all go to the mall!" said Nicoletta. "That would be fun." She clapped her hands like a moron and twirled to make her hair fly out in a golden cloud.

Christo was truly in love. Anything Nicoletta said sounded heavenly to him. "Great idea," he said. He ran his hand up her shoulder and caught at her thick, blonde hair. "You're already in your coat. Were you just leaving with the girls?"

"Yes," said Nicoletta.

Cathy and Rachel looked confused.

"We were talking about Anne-Louise," said Nicoletta. Cathy and Rachel were even more confused.

Christo, however, thought that Nicoletta was a wonderful, generous, and truly forgiving person. He could not get over how easily she had accepted Anne-Louise's presence in the

Madrigals, and how well she had dealt with her own loss. He complimented her profusely on her greatness of heart.

Cathy and Rachel looked skeptical.

Christo actually wanted to know if, on the way to the mall, they should swing by Anne-Louise's and pick her up and bring her along. "So the whole gang is together," he said eagerly, as if Nicoletta were part of the gang. Rachel cringed. Cathy held her breath. Boys were so thick.

"Sure," said Nicoletta. "I'd love to get to know her better." *Who is saying these things?* she thought. *The only thing I'd love to do right now is shake you off, Christo, so I can find Jethro.*

They clambered into the van. Christo turned the radio up higher, and then they talked louder, and he turned the radio up even more, and then they shouted and laughed and the interior of the van was a ringing cacophony of music and talk and giggling.

Nicoletta thought of unrequited love. It was dreadful. She could not believe she was a part of it. And yet, it was not unrequited, because Christo did not know. Once he knew, it would qualify. *I'm sorry, Christo,* she thought.

And then she heard the radio.

The update.

" . . . get a pizza," said Christo, taking Nicoletta's hand. "A new brick-oven pizzeria opened down by the highway exit. Want to go?"

" . . . rather go to the movies later on," said Cathy. "Let's all go, the way we used to. There's a fabulous fantastic cop-chase comedy playing."

Their voices were jackhammers in Nicoletta's skull.

" . . . rescue efforts," said the radio, "are to no avail. The fate of the two missing hunters remains unknown. On the economic front . . ."

"Isn't that scary?" shrieked Rachel. "I mean, those guys just walked off the face of the earth."

Walked off the face of the earth.

It was true. They had. The hunters had fallen down the gullet of the earth, and lay within its bowels.

"I wasn't inviting you for pizza, Cath-Cath," said Christo, friendly and flirty as ever. "Just Nicoletta." He smiled sweetly at Nicoletta and she ducked, as if the smile were a missile.

I was there when they walked off the face of it, she thought. *I know where the face of the earth ends*. And Jethro — what does he do? Cross the boundaries? Go between the face of the earth and whatever lies beyond?

The van whipped on well-plowed roads toward the city and the mall. Suddenly she saw the little dead-end road, and felt as if her eyes were being ripped out of her head in their effort to see all the way down it, and through the woods, and into the face of the cliff, and down the falling, falling cave.

"Nickie and I had the weirdest adventure the other night," said Christo, laughing and pointing. He turned down the volume of the radio and addressed the other girls. "We were going to park down at the end of that road. It dead-ends, you know, in a forest."

"We know," said Rachel in a sultry voice, implying that she, too, had parked a hundred times. Everybody laughed at her.

"Well," said Christo, in an introductory voice, as if he had much to say. "We go running through the woods. Nick and I. In the middle of the night! Ice and snow and moonshine. And we're running. Past boulders and trees and icicles hanging from the sky."

"Icicles hanging from the sky?" said Cathy, pretending to gag. "Christo you are getting altogether too romantic here. Next thing you know, you'll be writing greeting cards."

"Nickie?" repeated Rachel incredulously. "In the woods after dark? Come on."

"Nicoletta loves the outdoors," Christo told her.

"Nicoletta?" said Rachel.

"And," said Christo, "we spotted a thing. A Bigfoot. A monster. A Yeti. Something."

"I'll bet," said Cathy, giggling. "If I were running around in the woods in the middle of the night in the snow, I'd be seeing monsters, too."

"I'm serious," said Christo. He pulled into Fairest Lane without slowing for the curve, and the van spun momentarily out of control. "Oops," said Christo, yanking it back. He missed a tree by inches.

What if we had been killed? thought Nicoletta. Jethro would never know what happened to me.

She sneaked a corner-of-the-eye look at Christo. He had an excited look to him; not a preconcert look, but a prefootball game look. He was an athlete right now.

A hunter.

She had thought he had been confused or too swept away in his emotions to retain the memory of the stone that danced with Nicoletta between the lakes. She had thought he'd forgotten the warts of sand that covered its humanoid features, and its hair like old bones of thin fingers. Instead he had been making plans.

Christo pulled into the driveway of a house so similar to Nicoletta's old one that for a moment she thought she had fallen backward two years, the way the hunters had fallen backward into their particular hole. He honked the horn in a lengthy musical rhythm that must have made the neighbors crazy. Especially the neighbors Nicoletta remembered. It was a Madrigals' call. The hunters, she thought. What were they originally hunting? Ducks? Deer? Did they have a call, too?

I must make Christo hunt *me*, she thought, not Jethro. Christo must not go back. I betrayed Jethro once before. I can't let it happen again.

Anne-Louise came running out, laughing. "Want to go to the mall with us?" shouted Christo. She signaled yes and ran back for her coat and purse. "So what I'm going to do," said Christo to his three passengers, "is go back there and catch it."

"Catch what?" said Rachel.

There, thought Nicoletta. I admitted it. It's Jethro.

"The thing," said Christo. "Bigfoot. The monster. Whatever it is."

Rachel and Cathy exchanged looks. Give-us-a-break looks. This-nonsense-is-annoying-us looks.

Good, thought Nicoletta. If they laugh at him enough, we can get away from it. We'll make him forget it. I have to make him forget it.

"Or shoot it," said Christo, his voice as relaxed as if he were deciding on a flavor of ice cream for a sundae. "Whatever."

Shoot it? Nicoletta's heart felt shot. It isn't an "it," she thought, it's Jethro, you can't shoot him, *I won't let you shoot him!*

"I'd be the only person in North America who ever actually caught one." Christo beat out a rhythm on the steering wheel with his fists. "What a trophy, huh? Can you imagine the television coverage? I bet there's not a TV show in America I couldn't get on." His grin was different now. Not the sweet tremulous smile of first love, but a hard calculating grin.

A hunter. Ready to hunt.

Anne-Louise came running out of the house.

"After I shoot it, I guess I could have it stuffed," mused Christo.

Nicoletta clung to the seat belt.

"Christo," said Rachel. "Enough. Anne-Louise thinks we are civilized and interesting. Talking about shooting monsters in the woods will not do."

But Cathy was interested. She leaned forward. She tapped Nicoletta's shoulder. "Did you see it, too, Nickie?" she whispered, as if "it" were there, and might overhear, and so she needed to be careful.

Anne-Louise climbed into the van and yanked the sliding door shut after her. The van rocked when it slammed. She sat down breathlessly in the back with Cathy and Rachel and then, recognizing the front seat passenger, cried, "Nicoletta! Oh, what a pleasure! I've heard so much about you!"

"Nice to see you, too," said Nicoletta.

Cathy said louder, "Did you see it, too, Nickie?"

"Yes," said Nicoletta frantically. "I said hi. Nice to have Anne-Louise along."

"The monster," said Cathy irritably.

"No," said Nicoletta. "I didn't see anything. Of course not. There wasn't anything to see. Christo was seeing shadows."

Christo was genuinely angry. "I was not! You actually touched it, Nickie. Remember? Right there by the water and the cliff? Before we fell in?"

"You guys were running around in the dark in the woods where there were cliffs to fall off and water to fall in?" shrieked Rachel. "That sounds like the most horrible night on earth. Christo, remind me never to go on a date with you."

"It was Nicoletta's idea," said Christo defensively. "She knows the people who live around there."

"Who?" demanded Rachel. "Who lives around there?"

Nicoletta tried to shrug. "Nobody. Nothing. There wasn't anybody there."

"There was so a monster!" said Christo. He was really annoyed that she was not backing his story up. "And there was a cave! You were there, Nickie. You know I'm not making it up."

"A cave?" said Anne-Louise. "I wonder if that's what happened to those poor hunters. Where is this cave?"

Nicoletta was colder than she had ever been in the ice and snow.

Anne-Louise put a heavy, demanding hand on Nicoletta's shoulder. "Where is this cave?" she repeated. "We must notify the authorities. Who is this friend of yours who lives near there? He must show the rescue teams where to look."

Nicoletta heard her voice climb an octave and become brittle and screamy. "Christo is just being silly, Anne-Louise. Keep going to the mall, Christo. I need to buy . . . I need to look for . . . I'm out of . . ."

But she could not think of anything she needed or was out of.

Except time.

Chapter 13

At the mall, the teenagers gathered around a large, slablike directory of stores and entertainments. Christo was giving orders. First, he decreed, Anne-Louise was to stop her noise about the authorities. This had nothing to do with the two missing hunters. He was not going to tell her where the cave was. It would not become her business until she saw him on television. He was going by himself tomorrow morning to capture it. It would be his personal trophy. Second, Cathy and Rachel were to stop nagging and asking questions and not believing him. Third, Nicoletta was to tell him Jethro's last name and phone number, so he could get in touch with this person who undoubtedly knew the woods best.

Cathy and Rachel said they didn't know what anybody else was going to do about Christo's sudden personality change into staff sergeant, but they personally were going to try on shoes. Good-bye. And they would be happy to see Christo again once he turned back into a fun person.

Anne-Louise said that if Nicoletta and Christo wanted to hunt monsters and leave hunters to their hideous deaths, it was on their consciences not hers, and she was looking for shoes, too. So there.

Nicoletta was thinking that although her grasp of local geography was not great, the rear mall parking lot might back onto the woods. She might be able to walk through from this end and find the path, the two lakes, and Jethro. She waved good-bye to the other three girls.

What do I think will happen if I find the cave? Do I think Jethro will explain this away. Do I believe there could be an explanation? Do I expect to haul the hunters' bodies up so they can be found, and meanwhile hide Jethro? Do I expect to bring Jethro home with me, in whatever form he exists today, and ask my parents to let him sleep on the living room couch for a few years?

The mall was its usual bland self. Nothing ever changed there. The shiny, dark floors, the softly sliding escalators, the windows full of shoes and toys, the people sitting beneath indoor trees eating frozen yogurt. For a moment Nicoletta did not know which world was more strange: the world of the cave or the mall.

Christo, however, was not bland. He was full of the hunt. His muscles, his stride, his speech — they all talked together. He wanted this capture. He wanted this television coverage. This fame. This triumph.

It came to her in an unusual moment of understanding that he was not only hunting the thing he had seen in the forest; he was also hunting Nicoletta herself.

He was going to bring her a trophy she could not refuse.

He was going to show off his physical prowess, not on the football field where she had never even bothered to look, but in the forest, which she had claimed to love.

It was deeply flattering. She could not prevent herself from basking in this. Christo — admired by every girl in town — Christo wanted to impress only Nicoletta.

And she, after all, was not thinking only of Jethro. She wanted to impress Christo right back. But later. Much later. Right now she had to get to Jethro first. Warn him. Save him. Keep him.

As if, she thought in another moment of unwanted clarity, as if Jethro is *my* trophy before he's Christo's trophy.

She could think of nothing to say that was not stupid. Let's get French fries. Let's go with the others and try on sneakers. Let's check out the new videos and T-shirts and perfumes and pizza toppings. This nonsense when Christo was saying: Let's shoot the monster. And stuff it. Let's go out there and get the thing. "You don't want to come," he assured her. "You'd get squeamish." He laughed a strong male laugh, full of plans and promises. "In the morning," said Christo, "I'll take my father's shotgun."

The hunters had had shotguns. And what had happened to them?

She had a third all-too-clear vision.

It was not Jethro she had to worry about. Jethro was safe. The cave was his and he knew it.

It was Christo — innocent, show-off, excited Christo.

What had happened to the hunters would happen to him. He, too, would fall forever down. If she let Christo go on this expedition, she would betray him as well. She knew the length and depth of the fall Christo would take. She knew where he would hit bottom.

She knew he would never come out.

Never again sing or play ball. Never flirt or grow old.

Now as she looked at Christo, he seemed infinitely desirable. Perfect in every way. A person the world must have, a person who must live out his life span.

Christo, looking down at her, saw emotion in her eyes. He saw desire and fear and hope but he read it as love. Not a wish that he would live, but a wish that he would be hers.

Right there in the blandness of the encircling mall, among tired mothers pushing strollers and bored teenagers sipping soda, he kissed her with the sort of passion reserved for movies. The sort of intensity that belonged on late night drama.

He was embracing her with a ferocity she did not expect from a Madrigal singer. Perhaps this was Christo the football player, perhaps she was a goalpost he was trying to reach.

But no. He was kissing with the ferocity of a hunter.

When it ended, people were smiling softly and indulgently, enjoying this glimpse of true love. Christo was dizzy, backlit with the glow of his crush on her. He pulled slightly back from her to admire her from a distance of several inches instead of eyelashes against eyelashes.

But Nicoletta only wondered if Jethro would ever kiss her like that.

The day passed as, unbelievably, all days do.

It was a fact of life that fascinated Nicoletta. Even the worst days draw to a close. Sometimes a day seems to have the potential of lying there forever, trapping its victims as if they were treads on a circling escalator. But it never happens. The shopping ends, the van brings you home. The sun goes down, and the table is set for supper.

She endured her family. She swallowed her meal. She stared at a television screen. She held a book on her lap.

Outside, the snow fell yet again. They had never had such a winter for snow. The wind picked up, singing its own songs, sobbing its own laments. It dug tunnels in the drifts, as if hunting for its own set of hidden bodies.

Nicoletta undressed for the night.

Naked, she examined her body. What body did Jethro possess, he of the sandy hands and the granite face?

If I wait till morning, she thought, Christo will already have left on his hunt.

So I cannot wait till morning.

Chapter 14

The night was young. She had heard that phrase and never understood it. But now at one in the morning, she knew the meaning. She ran easily over the crusted snow, jumping the immense piles the plows had shoved against the curbs. She, too, was young. They had been born together, she and the night.

But the dirt road was far and the roads, with their walls of hard-packed, exhaust-blackened snow, obstructed her.

She was afraid of being seen. If a police car happened by . . . if grown-ups returning from parties noticed her . . . would they not stop? Demand to know why a lone girl was running down deserted streets at such an hour?

But the snow loaned Nicoletta enough hiding places to last a lifetime. Every pair of headlights caused her to bend a knee, and wait patiently behind a snow mountain until the vehicle passed by, and then she rose to her feet and ran on.

The night grew older. After one it became two, and was fast reaching three when finally she came to the end of the paved road, and found herself in the woods she wanted. She was exhausted. When the running ended, the trembling of legs and joints began, as if her body wanted to give up now, before its goal.

The boulder waited for her. It had gained in stature, for the snow had drifted upon it, increasing its height and breadth. As she trudged wearily up to it, snow fell from its stony mouth like words she did not comprehend.

She stopped walking. She had a sense of the boulder taking aim.

The moon was only a sliver, and the stars were diamond dust.

It was not enough to see by. And yet she saw.

And was seen.

In the pure, pure black of the night, she felt eyes. A thousand eyes, searching her like a thousand fingers. "Jethro," she whispered.

She wet her lips for courage and the damp froze and her mouth was encrusted with ice, the way Jethro's body was encrusted with sand. "Jethro," she cried, louder.

There was not a breath of wind. Just icy air

hunched down against the floor of the forest as if it planned not to shift for months. She waded through the cold and it hung onto her pants legs and shot through the lining of her jacket.

When she reached the boulder, she put her mittened hand against it for support. But there was no support. There was not even any rock. She fell forward, her hand arriving nowhere at all. She screamed, remembering her brief fall in the cave.

But this fall, too, was brief.

There was so much snow that her arm went through white right up to the elbow and then she touched rock. But under its blanket, the rock was not warm and friendly. It seemed to lunge forward, as if to hurtle her away from itself.

"Jethro!" she shrieked.

The trees leaned closer and listened harder. She pressed her back against the great rock, even though it did not want to shelter her. "Jethro!"

Her voice was the only sound in the silent black. It lay like an alien in another atmosphere. Nothing answered.

She would have to go to the cave in this terrible dark.

She remembered that first portion of her life when every day she had acted out *Little House on the Prairie.* She preferred being Laura, of course, because Laura had more fun, but every now and then it was her turn to be Mary. Nicoletta had always wanted to change the course of history and give Mary antibiotics so she didn't go blind. That was the only really awful thing in *Little House.* Oh, you could have your best friend read aloud to you for ten minutes and be your eyes for half an hour, but then you lost interest and had better things to do, and you didn't really like to think about Mary being stuck inside herself. Caught there in the dark. It used to make Nicoletta feel guilty and crawly that she could run away from blindness. Run into the sun and see and know the shapes and colors of the world, while Mary had to sit quietly at the table, forever and ever and ever in the dark.

The woods were so very dark.

She even thought she understood the meaning of forever, it was that dark.

If she did not find Jethro, she might lose her balance and slide into the black lakes and she, too, would be forever and ever in the dark.

A hand took hers firmly and guided her down the straight path toward the lakes. She was grateful for help and tightened her grip on the hand and even said thank you.

But there was no one there.

She was holding a stick. She could not even remember picking it up. It was weirdly forked, as if it really had once been a hand. She threw it hard into the trees to get it off her but it clung to her mitten and went nowhere. She began to cry soundlessly, because she was afraid the rest of the twigs and trees would attack if she made an ugly noise.

"Don't be afraid." The voice came from nowhere, from nothing. Now she screamed silently, twice as afraid. "They're trying to help," it said.

She was frozen. She had neither breath nor blood.

"It's me. I don't want you to look. I don't want you to know. You shouldn't have come, Nicoletta. Why do you keep coming when I keep telling you to stay away?"

Jethro. Oh, Jethro! "I had to warn you." She could not see anything. She knew his voice but he was not there. Nothing was there.

"Warn me of what?"

"Christo is coming back in the morning," she said. She began to cry again, and it was a mistake, for the tears froze separately on her cheeks and lay like rounded crystals upon her skin. "He wants to get you. Shoot you. Stuff you. He wants to take you for a trophy and go on television with you."

"Don't worry." Jethro's voice was consoling and gentle. "He won't find me. He'll find only the bottom of the cave."

The bottom of the cave.

Handsome, flirty, athletic Christo taking one step too many. Tumbling backward, screaming his final scream, hands flailing to stop himself, body twisting as helplessly as a pinecone falling from a tree.

Landing on the sharp spikes of stalagmites, dying slowly perhaps, his bones mingled with the bones of the hunters.

Oh, Christo! You don't deserve that!

He'll find only the bottom of the cave. How could Jethro say a thing of such horror in a voice of such comfort?

Fireworks of shock rocketed behind her blind eyes.

"Anyway," said Jethro, "the hunters will be glad to see him. They need company."

"What do you mean? Weren't they killed?"

"No one is killed by a fall into that cave."

"Jethro! Then I have to call the police! And the fire department! They'll bring ladders and ropes! We'll get the hunters out! We'll — "

"No, Nicoletta. No one gets out of the cave."

"You get out!"

"It took me a hundred years to learn how."

Exaggeration annoyed her. "Don't be ridiculous. Jethro, where are you? I can't really see you."

"I don't want you to really see me," he said quietly. "I don't want you to be as scared of me as you would be."

"I've seen you before! I know you in that shape. Jethro, *I need you.*"

There was no sound in the woods except the sound of her own breathing. Perhaps Jethro did not breathe. Perhaps he was all rock and no lungs. But then, how did he speak? Or did he not? Was she making it up? Was she out here in the woods by herself, talking to trees, losing her mind?

"You need me?" said Jethro. His voice quavered.

Humans have two great requirements of life. To be needed is as important as love. Now she knew that he was human, that he was the boy who sat beside her in art as well as the creature wrapped in stone. "I need you," she repeated. She slid her scarlet mitten off her hand and extended her bare fingers into the night.

The hand that closed around them rasped with the rough edges of stone. But the sob that came from his chest was a child's.

Chapter 15

They sat on the boulder, wrapped in snow as
if in quilts. It was a high, round throne and the
woods were their kingdom. The night was old
now. The silver sliver of moon had come to rest
directly above them, and its frail light gleamed
on the old snow and shimmered on her gold
hair.

She kept his hands in her lap like possessions. They were real hands. They had turned
real between her own, as if the oven of her
caring had burnt away the bad parts. "You are
a real boy," she said to him.

"I was once. It was a long time ago."

She snuggled against him as if expecting a
cozy bedtime story of the sort her parents loved
to tell.

"Long ago," said Jethro. He told his story
in short spurts, letting each phrase lie there in
the dark, as if each must mellow and grow old

like the night before he could go on to the next. "Long before the Pilgrims," said Jethro, "ancient sailors from an ancient land shipwrecked here."

The town was only a few miles from the sea, but she never thought of it that way. There was no public beach and Nicoletta rarely even caught a glimpse of the ocean. People with beaches were people with privacy.

"They found the cave," said Jethro slowly, "and explored it for gold."

Yes. She could believe that. Those gleaming walls and incredible patterns of royal rock — anybody would expect to find treasure.

"There was none. The men who went first fell to the bottom, and could not be rescued by the others." His voice waited until she had fully imagined the men in the bottom who could not be rescued. "They had to be abandoned," he said, his voice a tissue of sorrow.

"Still alive?" asked Nicoletta.

"Still alive."

Wounded and broken. Screaming from the bottom of a well of blackness. Hearing no words of comfort from above. But instead, words of farewell. *We're sorry, we have to go now. Die bravely.*

"In their society," said Jethro, "the soul could not depart from the body unless the body was burned at sea with its ship. But they, of course, could never return to the ship. And so the men at the bottom of the cave never died. Their souls could not leave. Their bodies . . . dissolved over the decades." His voice was soft. With revulsion or pity, she did not know. "Until," he said, "they became the cave itself. Things with warts of sand and crusts of mineral."

His hands took her golden hair, and he wove his fingers through it, and then he kissed her hair, kissed that long thick rope, but he did not kiss her face. "The ones who fell," said Jethro, "put a curse on the cave."

A chill of horrified excitement flashed down Nicoletta's spine. She had never heard a human being utter those words. *A curse be upon you.*

"What was the curse?" She whispered because he did. Their voices were hissing and lightweight, like falling snow.

"Whoever entered that cave," said Jethro, "would be forever abandoned by the world. Just as they had been."

Was he one of them? Ancient as earth? But the boy she knew from Art was her age. A breathing, speaking boy with thick, dark hair and hidden eyes.

"And did Indians fall in?" she asked.

"The Indians always had a sense of the earth

and its mysteries. They knew better than to go near the cave."

He seemed to stop. He seemed to have nothing more to say. She asked no questions. The moon slid across the black, black sky. "Then," said Jethro, "white men came again to these shores. To farm and hunt and eventually to explore." Now he was speaking with difficulty, and the accents of his voice were lifting and strange. "My father and I," he said, "found the cave. So beautiful! I had never seen anything beautiful. We did not have a beautiful life. We did not have beautiful possessions. So I stayed in the outer chambers, touching the smooth rock. Staring at the light patterns on the brimstone. Dazzled," he said. "I was dazzled. But my father . . ."

How softly, how caressingly, he spoke the word *father*. A shaft of moonlight fell upon the monstrous shape of him and she could see the boy inside the rock. His eyes might have been carved from a vein of gold. He smiled at her, the sculpture of his face shifting as if it lived. It was a smile of ineffable sadness.

"My father went on in."

She turned to look at him.

"My father fell, of course. He fell among the abandoned, and they kept him."

He stopped. The warmth of the great rock

dissipated. It was cold. She waited for Jethro to descend through the centuries and return to her.

"I didn't leave the cave. If I had run back out . . . things would have been different. But I loved my father," he said. His voice broke. "I offered myself in exchange. I told the spirits at the bottom of the cave that they could have me if they would give up my father. They were willing. My father was willing. He said he would come back for me. He emerged at the same moment that I fell into the cave on purpose."

Jethro paused for a long time. "I try to remember that," he told Nicoletta. "I try to remember that I stepped off the edge because I wanted to."

"Were you hurt?"

He smiled again, his sadness so great that Nicoletta wept when he did not. "I broke no bones," he said finally. He said it as if something else had broken.

"What did your father do? He must have run back to the house and the town and gotten everybody to brings ropes and ladders."

Jethro's smile was not normal. "There was a curse on the cave," he said. "I told you that." His words seemed trapped by the frost. They hung in front of his lips, crystallized in the air.

She had been listening to the story without listening. It was a problem for her in school, too. She heard but did not keep the teachers' words. She moved her mind backward, to retrieve Jethro's speech. *"Whoever entered,"* she repeated slowly, *"would be forever abandoned by the world. Just as they had been."*

Jethro nodded.

The moon was hidden by a cloud.

Jethro put a hand gently over her eyes. "Don't move," he said softly. "Don't look again."

His hand was heavy. Stonelike. "Your father?" she said. "Abandoned you?"

"He walked away. He walked out of the cave and into the daylight. He never came back. Nobody ever came back. I called and called. Day after day I called. He was my father! He loved me. I know he did. Even though there was nothing else beautiful in our lives, that was beautiful. He loved me."

She opened her eyes under the weight of his hands and saw only the underside of a rock. She closed her eyes again.

"Even though I gave myself up for him," said Jethro, his voice caught as if it, too, were falling to a terrible fate, "I didn't understand that it was forever. I was sure he would return and rescue me."

Rescue. A lovely word. Certain and sure. I will rescue you, Jethro, thought Nicoletta. I love you. I will rescue you from all curses and dark fallings.

"But he didn't, of course," said Jethro.

Jethro cried out. A strange terrible moan like the earth shifting. A groan so deep and so long she knew that he was still calling for his father to rescue him.

Being a monster was not as terrible as being abandoned by his father. Nothing on earth could be worse. Forgotten by your father? A child goes on loving a father who drinks too much, or beats him, or does drugs . . . but a father who leaves the son to endure horror forever . . . and even forgets that he did that . . . it was the ultimate divorce.

Abandoned. The word took on a terrible force. She could see his feet — that father's feet — as they walked away. Never to turn around. She could hear the cries, echoing over the years: that son, calling his father's name. Never to hear an answer.

"I try not to hate him," said Jethro. "I try to remember that there were no choices for him. The curse carried him away from me and kept him away. But he was my father!" The voice rose like the howl of a dying animal into the winter air. "He was my father! I thought he would come! I waited and waited and waited."

The voice sagged, and fell, and splintered on the forest floor.

"Oh, Jethro!" she said, and hugged him. He was sharp and craggy but the tighter she held her arms the more he softened. She felt him becoming the boy again, felt the power of her caring for him fight the power of the curse upon him. He removed his heavy hand from her eyes but she kept them closed for a while anyhow.

"You can emerge from the cave and be a real person some of the time," she said.

"It's a gift of the light. Sunlight, usually. I am surprised that the moonlight is giving me this now. Sunshine is a friend. It doesn't end the curse, but sometimes it gives me a doorway to the world. Haven't you noticed that I am only in school on sunny days? I cannot touch the world except on bright days."

"I will make all your days bright," said Nicoletta.

"You have," he said, his voice husky with emotion. "I think of you when I cannot leave."

For a long time they sat in each other's arms. Moonlight glittered on the fallen snow and danced on the icy fingers of trees. Very carefully she turned to look at him. He was Jethro. She sighed with relief. He had been in there all along, and she — she, Nicoletta Storms — had freed him with her presence. "At least I'll see you in school," she said.

"No. I can't go again."

"Why not? *Why not?* You have to! Oh, Jethro, you have to come back to school! I have to see you!" She gripped his arms and held him hard.

"You must forget about me."

"I can't. I won't. You don't want me to. I don't want to. We're not going to forget about each other."

He said nothing.

"Why do you come to school?" she asked him.

"To dream of how it might have been. You are my age. The age, anyway, that I was once. The age when I fell. I hear human voices, I recognize laughter. I see human play and friendship."

Oh, the loneliness of the dark!

She pictured her family. How loving they were. How warm the small house was. She thought of Jethro, returning every time to the dark and the rage of the trapped undead. She kissed him, hungrily, to kiss away his loss. Around them the trees leaned closer and looked deeper. "Jethro, if feels as if the woods are alive," she whispered.

"They are," said Jethro. "We were all something else once. Every tree and stone. Every lake and ledge."

Horror surrounded her. She breathed it into her lungs and felt it crawl into her hair, like bats. She could not look into the woods.

"You must go home. You must never come again."

"But I love you."

He flinched. He pushed her away, and then could not bear that, because nobody had loved him in so very long. He held her more tightly than ever, cherishing the thought. *Somebody loved him.*

Love works only when it circles, and it *had* circled. It had enclosed them both. She loved him and he loved her back. He had to love her enough to make her stay away.

"Never come near the cave again. They know about you. They will look for you now, and guide your steps so that you fall. They will take you, Nicoletta. What else do they have to do for all eternity? Nothing. They will never be buried by fire at sea. You must go and never come back."

She was unmoved. Nobody would tell her never to do anything. Nobody would tell her that she could find true love and then have to walk away from it! No. She would always come back.

"Nicoletta," he said. His voice was hollow now, like a reed . . . or a cave.

"If you get too close, not only will you fall, I — cursed by the cave — I would do to you what my own father did to me."

She was looking into his eyes, eyes like precious gemstones. I love you, she thought.

He said, *"I would abandon you."*

Abandon her? She could not believe it. He loved her. Love did not abandon.

"Abandon you forever, Nicoletta. In the dark. Turning to stone. Forgotten. I would not come back. Nobody would ever come back for you."

The moon hid behind wispy clouds. The night was too old to be called night. Jethro left. He had been there, and then he was not. She was alone on the stone in the dark.

For he did love her.

And to prove it, he had to leave. And so did she.

Chapter 16

It had taken great courage to walk into the woods.

It took none to walk out.

If Jethro was not afraid of what the trees and ledges had once been, how could she be afraid? She said good-bye to the boulder, but it said and did nothing, which surprised her. She had expected a response after the conversation and the agony it had heard; the loving it had seen.

When she reached the paved road, she would have to put away these things. Enter into her other life.

How distant it seemed — her other world.

Nicoletta touched the pavement.

Dawn was coming. Quickly the sun threw scarlet threads into the sky, and quickly the snow turned pink in greeting. As if they were flirting and blushing. Like me, she thought.

She smiled to herself, and then smiled at the sun.

She walked swiftly. She was happy.

What is there to be happy about? she thought. That the sun rises? That I love Jethro but he doesn't want me to come again?

And yet she was happy in a liquid way, as if she were still all one, a water glass of pure happiness, a crystal cylinder of delight.

Love, she thought. I know what it is now. It's every molecule of you. It connects you to yourself, even if you cannot be connected to the person who caused it.

Jethro. Oh, it was a beautiful name!

A car turned down the DEAD END road.

She had not wanted the other world to appear so soon.

A second vehicle followed it.

She considered hiding. Stepping off the road into the trees. She knew that the trees would take her in. Circle her, and blind the cars to her presence for Jethro's sake. Snow, its sides packed like a ski jump by a plow, and a little, green holly tree without berries were on either side of her. She could hunch down behind the sharp, leather leaves and not be seen.

The first vehicle was Christo's van. The second vehicle was a television network van.

Nicoletta had omitted the part that counted.

She had entertained herself. She had run to Jethro for talk and love and comfort and daydreams. But the important part of what she had needed to do before morning, she had skipped.

Christo, who was equally liquid and crystal with love. Christo, who was hot and surging with the need to show off, to hunt, to capture or to destroy.

Not only had Christo come. He had brought teams. Witnesses. Camera film. And, no doubt, weapons.

She thought of the cave. The long fall that Christo and his TV crew would take. The horrible slime and sand and narrowing walls of shining stone. The knowledge that they were doomed. Of course, they would not have that knowledge as they fell. They would think there was a way out. Or that rescue would come.

How many days, or weeks . . . *or years* . . . would they struggle against their fate? How long before they became, as Jethro had become, part of the cave? Just another outcropping of sand and rock and dripping water? Would she, Nicoletta, in that other world have grown up and had children and grandchildren and been buried herself by the time Christo understood and surrendered to his fate?

The van rushed down the narrow road.

143

Christo drove too fast, gripping the wheel of his car, leaning forward as if trying to see beyond the windshield and through the woods, behind the rock and into the cave. He looked neither left nor right, only ahead. He didn't see the packed snow and the holly, let alone Nicoletta. She had a glimpse of his profile as he sped past. How handsome he was. How young and perfect.

And how excited. He thought this would be an adventure. And oh! it would be. But not one in which he conquered.

She could not let him fall! Nor could she let those poor strangers in the van meet that fate.

The television van came much more slowly. Its driver was middle-aged and frowning, studying the road, the snow, the sky, as if he were worrying about a change in the weather, the studio deadline, his taxes, his wife, and his aching feet all at the same time.

He could have been her father.

He was surely somebody's father. Would he, like the hunters, end up forever fallen?

I have to do something, she thought. But what? I can't talk them out of it. The more information I give them, the more eager they'll be. The more I explain, the quicker they'll rush to see for themselves. And even if they stay away from the cave, even if I can convince them to stay in the meadow, or between the lakes, or among the trees . . . they'll try to shoot Jethro.

I have no control. I have no moves. I have no way to turn.

This is not the world of the ancient Indians who understood that there were mysteries, and that mysteries should not be touched. This is the world of the television networks, who think that everything on earth belongs to them and ought to be captured on their cameras.

Perhaps she owed Christo nothing; after all, she did not love him; it was he who loved her. Perhaps she should let them go, and let Jethro control what happened.

But love was too precious. Even if it was not hers, and would never be hers, how could she be part of its ending? She did not love Christo, but it counted that he loved her.

The television van was almost upon her.

She flung herself out from behind the piled snow and the little holly tree . . . directly under the wheels of the van.

"She jumped!" said the van driver constantly. "I swear it. The girl jumped right in front of me."

"I slipped," Nicoletta explained. It was not easy to talk because of the pain. The broken leg was so very broken. Pieces of bone stuck out of her flesh like long white splinters. "Snow," she explained. "Ice. No sand on the road yet. It's my fault. I should have been more careful."

Whatever spell Christo had cast to coax a network to send a crew, had dried up. The people who had been eager to film whatever this kid thought he'd seen, especially since it was near the disappearing point of the two hunters, were now interested in nothing but getting through a terrible day. The van driver was desperate to be sure everybody understood it was not his fault. He said this to Nicoletta's parents and to the doctors and the admitting secretary in the emergency room and to Christo.

Christo had questions of his own to ask Nicoletta, but being severely hurt provided its own camouflage. She need only close her eyes, rest her long lashes on her pale cheeks, and whisper. "I'm tired, Christo, visit me tomorrow." And he had to leave. No options.

The cast was big and white and old-fashioned. No vinyl and metal athletic brace for a break this bad; solid heavy-duty plaster and bandage was like a rock attached to her leg. She had always rather hoped to be wearing a cast one day, and attract lots of sympathetic attention, and have to use crutches.

But now she faced a new nightmare.

How will I go back to Jethro? thought Nicoletta. I can't get through the woods with this. I can't use crutches in the snow.

Not only had she stopped Christo and the TV crew from looking for Jethro, she had stopped herself.

People asked what she had been doing, anyway, on some remote road at the crack of dawn? There was only one acceptable excuse and she used it. "I've taken up jogging, you know. I've been running every morning."

Her parents had not known this, but then, they didn't get up before dawn and could not say she hadn't been.

Jamie was too jealous of the attention Nicoletta was getting to ask difficult questions. Jamie kept looking around for cute interns instead.

When Nicoletta woke up in the afternoon, she was alone in a quiet hospital room with pastel walls. The other bed was empty. There was something eerie about the flat white sheets and the untouched, neatly folded, cotton blanket on the other bed. It was waiting for its next victim.

The door was closed. She had no sense of noise or action or even human beings around her. She might have been alone at the bottom of the cave, she was so alone in the bare, pale room.

Her leg hurt.

Her head ached.

I'll never even be able to tell Jethro what I did for him, she thought, in a burst of self-pity. I'll hobble around by myself and nobody will care.

The door was flung open, banging heavily into the pastel plaster wall.

The Madrigals burst into the room, singing as they came. It was so corny. They were singing an old European hiking song: "And as we go, we love to sing, our knapsacks on our backs. Foll-der-oolllll, foll-der-eeeeee, our knapsacks on our backs."

She was so glad to see them that it made her cry. It was hokey, but it was beautiful. It was friendship.

"Now, now," said Ms. Quincy, "we won't stay long, it's too exhausting for somebody as badly hurt as you are. We just wanted you to be sure you know that you're among friends."

Nicoletta looked up, thinking, Ms. Quincy had a lot of nerve, when she'd kicked Nicoletta away from those friends. But out loud she said, "Hi, everybody. I'm glad to see you."

They all kissed her, and Christo's kiss was

no different from anybody else's. She wanted to catch his hand, and see if he was all right. Ask what he was thinking. But she didn't really want to know.

Rachel had brought colored pens so everybody could sign the cast. Rachel herself wrote, *"I love you, Nickie! Get well soon!"*

This meant everybody could write, *I love you, Nickie,* and they did. David and Jeff, whom she hardly knew, wrote, *"I love you, Nickie, get well soon."* Cathy did, Lindsay did, even Anne-Louise. *"Love you, Nickie!"*

Christo was last. She had to do something. She was out of action, but he might return to the cave anyway. She had to exert some sort of pull on him.

"Why were you there?" he breathed. "What were you doing? It was awfully far from home to be jogging."

"I knew you were coming, Christo," she murmured. "I wanted to watch you in action. I wanted to be part of it." She squeezed his hand. "Promise me you won't do anything unless I'm along to watch you, Christo?"

Everything about him softened. The love he had for her surfaced so visibly that the girl Madrigals were touched and the boy Madrigals were embarrassed. Nicoletta blushed, but not from love. Because he believed her. Because love, among all the other things it was, was gullible. Everybody had written, "Love you, Nickie," but he wrote on her cast, *"I love you more. Christo."*

The Madrigals left, singing again, this time a burbling Renaissance song that imitated brooks and flutes. It was a lullabye, and Nicoletta slept, deep and long.

She dreamed that she was falling.

Falling in dreadfully icy cold, wind whipping through her hair and freezing her lungs. She dreamed that her hand was reaching for something to catch. Anything! A branch, a rock, a ladder, a rope —

— but found only sand.

The flat of her palm slid across the grit, finding nothing to hold, nothing at all, and the black forever hole below her opened its mouth.

In her sleep she screamed silently, because everything in that terrible world was dark and silent, and in one last desperate try she tightened her grip.

She found a hand. It held her. It saved her. She woke. It was Jethro's hand. He had come. He was safe. He had not been hurt, and nobody had hurt him. He was here in a pastel hospital room.

He leaned over her bed and found her lips. He kissed her as lightly as air and whispered,

"Nicoletta. *Oh, Nicoletta.* I love you."

Even when used by strangers like David and Jeff, or people at whom she was angry like Ms. Quincy, those three words remained beautiful. But from the lips of the boy she loved, those three words were the most beautiful on earth.

"I love you, too," she whispered.

A rare smile illuminated his face, momentarily safe from its terrible burdens. They held hands, and his was graveled and rasping, and hers was soft and silken.

Chapter 17

Jethro yelled at Nicoletta, albeit softly. "You could have been killed!"

"I know that now, but there wasn't time to think of that then."

"What were you thinking of?" he demanded.

"You."

The quiet of the hospital room deepened, and the pale colors of the walls intensified. Her hand in his felt warmer and his hand in hers felt gentler. "I can't stay long," he said.

"Why not? Stay forever."

He smiled sadly. He understood what forever meant. She had no grasp.

"Then I'll talk fast. Jethro, I have ideas." Her eyes burned with excitement. "The thing is," she said, "to bury them. Right?"

"To bury them?" repeated Jethro.

"The ancient souls! They didn't get buried. That's the problem, right? So we have to bury them. We'll blast the cave! We'll dynamite them up! Or else we'll flood the cave! Or else we'll bring torches. We'll get toy wooden boats to count as their ships and set fire to those!"

He did not respond.

"Jethro! Don't you think those ideas are terrific?"

He said instead, "Who do you think you will have if you have me?"

Now she was the one to repeat words that meant nothing to her. "Who will I have if I have you?"

"Nicoletta," he said. "What if you have me . . . as a thing?"

She did not want to think about that.

"You screamed the first time I touched you. Because I am part of the cave. It's in me now. I don't even know why I came here, I could get caught in my other shape. There's no way out of my other being, Nicoletta." His sentences, normally so hard to come by, tumbled and fell on top of each other, like hunters in caves. "You told me yourself what your friend Christo wanted to do to me. Shoot me. Or exhibit me."

"Well, I won't let him."

"How many times do you plan to step in front of trucks?"

After the fact, Nicoletta was aware of what

she had done. She certainly did not want death. That was what this was all about! She wanted life, and she wanted it for both of them. Life and love, hope and joy. No. She did not plan to step in front of any more trucks. "Jethro, there has to be a way out for us."

His eyes looked into a deep distance she could not follow. Did not want to follow. Did not want to think about. "Think of rescue," she said urgently. "We have to work on this, Jethro." She gripped him with both her hands. "What's the point of love if we can't be together?"

His chest rose and fell. She wanted his shirt off, so she could touch his skin and rest her cheek against that beating heart.

His lips moved silently, but she could not read the words. Was he repeating that lovely word *rescue*? Was he imagining that it really could be done? That there really was a way out?

He said, "Love always has a point. Even if it stays within. Or is hidden. Or is helpless."

Nicoletta was angry with him. That was stupid. Who would want a helpless love? Who would want a hidden love?

"Okay," she said, "if you don't want to try anything drastic, what we'll do is tell my parents. We'll explain. They're wonderful people. We'll — "

"And think of what could go wrong," he interrupted. "What if your father fell into the cave? Or your mother? Or your little sister? To be lost forever instead?"

She wanted to joke. My little sister wouldn't be such a loss. But he knew nothing of jokes. "You don't even want to try dynamite?" she said.

"How would you get it?"

"My father bought some to blow up stumps in the backyard. But he never got around to it. It's just there in the garage."

He shook his head. The silence she had first found fascinating annoyed Nicoletta now. "We have to work out a strategy!" she said sharply. "We need to make plans."

But he said nothing, keeping his thoughts. Her hospital room darkened, more infected by his bleak hopelessness than her eager love.

A nurse bustled into the room. She was the sort of woman who called her patients "we." "How are we feeling, dear?" she said, thrusting a thermometer into Nicoletta's mouth so that answers were not possible. "Let's take our blood pressure," she said. She pumped the cuff up so tightly on Nicoletta's arm that Nicoletta had to hold her breath to keep from crying. She did not want to be a sissy in front of Jethro. She stayed in control by trying to read her blood pressure upside down, watching the mercury bounce on the tiny dial. She failed. "What is it?" she asked the nurse.

"Fine," said the nurse. "Keep the thermometer in your mouth."

"But what were the numbers?" mumbled Nicoletta. She hated medical people who kept your own bodily facts to themselves.

Reluctantly, as if answering might start a riot, the nurse said, "One-ten over seventy."

Nicoletta, who had studied blood pressure in biology last year, was delighted. "I'm in great health then," she said happily. The thermometer fell out of her mouth and onto the sheets. The nurse picked it up grumpily. Then she placed two cool fingers on Nicoletta's wrist.

Nicoletta looked at Jethro to share amusement at an old-fashioned nurse. Jethro was not there. A thing, a dark and dripping thing, like a statue leaking its own stone, was propped against the wall. Crusted as if with old pus, it could have been a corpse left to dry.

A scream rose in Nicoletta's throat. Horror as deep as the cave possessed her. He had changed right there, right in this room. In public, in front of people, he had become a monster. She could not look at him, she could not bear it that beautiful Jethro had turned into this.

"My goodness!" exclaimed the nurse. "Your pulse just skyrocketed. Whatever are you thinking about?"

I cannot scream, she thought. People will come. The nurse just has to leave quietly with her little chart and her little cart. I cannot scream.

She screamed.

The nurse followed Nicoletta's eyes and saw a monster.

In the split second before the nurse, too, screamed in horror, Nicoletta saw Jethro's eyes hidden beneath the oozing grit of his curse. Shame and hurt filled his eyes like tears. Fear followed, swallowing any other emotions.

Jethro was terrified.

Oh, Jethro! she thought. Your life isn't a life, it's a nightmare. Your body isn't a body, it's a trap.

Jethro vanished from the room before the nurse could finish reacting. Nicoletta heard his steps, lugging himself out of the room, down the hall, trying to escape.

There was nothing left of him there but a gritty handprint on a pastel wall.

The nurse was made of stronger stuff than Nicoletta had thought. She caught her scream and ran out of the room after Jethro, shouting for security.

No, thought Nicoletta, let him get away! Please let him get away!

She needed to run interference, needed to make excuses, think up lies, anything! Her leg lay on the mattress, heavy and white and unmoving. She literally could not get off the bed.

"Okay, okay," said a grumpy voice in the hallway outside Nicoletta's door, "We've phoned for security. Somebody will be up in a few minutes. Now what was the intruder doing?"

There was a pause. Nicoletta recognized it. The nurse had no idea what to say without sounding ridiculous or hysterical. "He was — he was just standing there," said the nurse lamely.

"What did he look like?" said the grumpy voice. "Race? Age?"

The nurse said nothing for a moment. Then she said, "I'm not sure. Ask the patient."

She's sure, thought Nicoletta. She knows what she saw. She saw a monster. But she can't say that. The words won't come out of her mouth.

Security never came in to ask Nicoletta anything. An aide, not the nurse, arrived later to finish charting Nicoletta's vital signs. Nicoletta said nothing about an intruder. The aide said nothing.

She thought of Jethro's journey home. How would he get there?

How could she ever refer to that cave as home?

Home. She knew now that a house was only a house; the building on Fairest Lane was a place to buy and sell, to decorate, and to leave. But a home is a place in which to be cherished. A home is love and parents, shelter and protection, laughter and chores, shared meals and jokes.

Home.

He had none.

And how with that curse upon him, could she bring him home? Find safety for him? Find release?

Her parents and Jamie burst into the room, loaded down with Nicoletta's schoolbooks and homework, a potted flower, a silly T-shirt from the hospital gift shop, and a balloon bouquet. The balloons rushed to the ceiling, dotting it purple and silver and scarlet and gold.

She wondered if Jethro had even seen a balloon bouquet. Or ever would.

"I'm so glad to see you!" cried Nicoletta. "Oh, Mommy! Daddy! Jamie!"

"You're even glad to see me?" said Jamie. "You *are* sick!"

"Darling," said her mother, hugging. "You look like you've had a good long nap. Feeling better?"

"Lots."

"You come home tomorrow," said her father. He looked worn and worried. He touched her cheek, as if to reassure himself that this was Nicoletta, his baby girl, his darling daughter.

"Tomorrow? I just got here." She thought of a father, years and years go, who left a son inside the earth and never looked back.

"Isn't it wonderful?" agreed her father. "Then just another day of rest at home and you're on crutches and back in school. Orthopedic decisions are very different from when I broke a leg. When I broke my leg skiing, back in the dark ages, why, I was in the hospital for ten days."

They talked about the dark ages: her parents' childhoods, in which there had been no fast food, no video games, no answering machines, and no instant replays.

Nicoletta thought of Jethro, for whom all ages were dark.

I know what I could do, she thought. I could do what Jethro did for his father. *I could offer myself to the spirits of the cave.* I could exchange myself for him.

How romantic that would be!

Greatness of heart would be required. She would step down and he would step up. She would take the dark and he could have the light.

Jethro would have his fair share of laughter and love; he would smile in the sun, with no fear of turning to horror and stone. He would have his chances, at last, for life, liberty, and the pursuit of happiness. The dark ages would end for him.

And she, Nicoletta . . . she . . . would inherit the dark ages.

Dark. Forever and ever, world without end.

Dark and all that. *dark* meant. Unknown. Unseen. Things that crawled and bit and flew and slithered. Things that crept up legs and settled in hair. Things that screamed and moaned and wept in the entrapment of their souls.

Could she really do that? Was she, Nicoletta, strong enough to accept darkness and terror, fear and slime — *forever*?

But it would not be forever, of course. He would come back for her. He would —

He would not.

He would not even remember. He would abandon her. Everybody would abandon her.

She thought of the Madrigals. How quickly they had abandoned her for Anne-Louise. She thought of Ms. Quincy, who had praised her voice for so long, only to abandon her the instant she heard a better one. It would all be like that, she thought. My entire life. Except my life would not have a span. It would not end. There would be no way out. It would be eternal.

Oh, Jethro! Jethro!

I don't want you caught in your dark ages. I want you here on earth with me.

"Sweetie, don't cry," said her mother. "It isn't that bad of a break. All will be well. I promise."

She rested on her mother's promise.

She thought of Jethro going back, and down, and in. To become part of the walls and the fall and the blackness, to live among the spirits he would not describe because they were too awful for her to hear about.

"Don't cry," said her mother, rocking. "All will be well."

Chapter 18

"A snow picnic?" repeated Nicoletta.

"Yes!" said Anne-Louise. "It was my idea. And you'll be our mascot!"

Your mascot? thought Nicoletta. I get it. You're the soprano, Anne-Louise. I'm the puppy. The rag doll. The mascot. Drop dead, Anne-Louise, just drop dead.

Christo said, "I'm driving!"

Rachel said, "I packed the sandwiches."

Cathy said, "But I made them, so don't be afraid of food poisoning, Nickie."

Nicoletta had to laugh. She got her crutches. Christo's van was not large enough for so many Madrigals, but if they really squished and squashed, they could fit in a very uncomfortable but delightful way. The three leftovers followed in a leftover car. Nicoletta felt sorry for them, trailing behind.

Her white packed leg with its scrawls of

Madrigal names stuck out in front of her, between the two bucket seats.

Christo said, "We're going to that meadow you showed me, Nick. I thought I might climb the cliff."

Anne-Louise gave a little shriek of fright. "Christo! You might fall!"

Christo smiled arrogantly. Falling happened to other climbers. Not to Christo.

"It'll be icy," warned Anne-Louise. She patted Christo's knee excitedly.

Nicoletta definitely knew who had a crush on whom. Well, it was useful in a way. Christo would be deflected. It would free Nicoletta up for Jethro.

"Okay, Nickie," said Rachel. "The time has come. What is this crazy story Christo keeps telling us about rock people?" The packed singers burst into laughter and the whole van shook.

Christo just grinned. "You'll stop laughing when I catch it," he said.

"Actually," Anne-Louise said, turning to speak clearly, and be sure everybody knew that she knew first, "Christo brought his gun. He's not going to climb. He's going to hunt."

"I'm against hunting," said Rachel.

"I usually am, too," said Cathy, "but this is a rock he's after. The worst that can happen,

I figure, is there'll be two rocks after he shoots at it."

Nicoletta's brain felt as solid as the cast on her leg. She had plaster in her skull. What was happening? The cave and Jethro were becoming public territory. There were no taboos, there was no fear, there was no stopping them now. Even Cathy was laughing about hunting. It occurred to Nicoletta that she could not pretend Jethro was against hunting.

In fact, he and his companions in the cave were the most vicious hunters of all. For they hunted the hunters.

"I want a souvenir," said Anne-Louise, in a little girl singsong voice.

Nicoletta hated her. She hated the flirting, the silliness, the fakery. She hated every single thing about Anne-Louise. Drop dead, she thought. Out loud she said, "It won't be any fun picnicking there, Christo. Let's go to the state park or the town lake."

"Forget it," said Cathy. "He's told us and told us about this place, how romantic and weird it is, what strange things we'll see. We're on. This is it, Nickie."

They turned into the lane that said DEAD END.

They drove past the few houses and the high, winter-tired hedges.

They drove right up the dirt road and came to stop where the ruts were too deep for a suburban van. "How will we ever get through all this snow?" cried Anne-Louise, pretending fear. "How will we ever find our way in those woods?"

"Not to worry," said Christo, comforting her. He was completely sucked in by her acting.

Nobody except Nicoletta seemed bothered by Anne-Louise. The altos, tenors, and basses piled out, the leftover car with its leftover people caught up, the boys hoisted the coolers and then they were faced with the problem of Nicoletta's cast and crutches.

"See?" said Nicoletta. "I really think the town lake would be a good idea. That way you can prop me up on a bench right near where we park, and we'll still have a good view, and yet we — "

"Nickie," said Rachel, "hush. The boys are going to carry you. This is the most romantic moment of your life, so enjoy it."

Christo and Jeff made a carrying seat of their linked arms and David helped her sit. With David holding her cast at the ankle as if she were a ladder he was lugging, Christo and Jeff carried her.

They went past the boulder.

Straight as folded paper, the path led them through the snow-crusted meadow. Weeds from last summer poked out of last week's snow, brown and dried and somehow evil. The weeds tilted, watching the trespassers.

The two lakes were free of ice. They lay waiting. Tiny waves lapped the two shores like hungry tongues.

"Ooooh, it's so pretty!" squealed Anne-Louise.

The sound of their crunching feet was like an army. Jethro was surely hidden safely away; he would have heard them coming.

I couldn't stop them! Nicoletta thought at Jethro. It isn't my fault! I wouldn't have come, but I have to keep an eye on them.

The air was silent and the cave was invisible. They stopped walking. Only Anne-Louise found the place pretty. Rachel swallowed and wet her lips. "The water looks dangerous," she whispered. "It looks — as if it wants one of us."

Nobody argued.

Nobody said she was being silly.

Nobody tried to walk between the two lakes, either.

The boys set Nicoletta down. They set the big cooler down, too, and Nicoletta used it for a chair.

Ice had melted on the side of the cliff, and

then frozen again. It hung in thin, vicious spikes from its crags and outcroppings. There was no color. The stone was dark and threatening. The day was grim and silent.

Christo's voice came out slightly higher than it should have. "I'm walking between the two lakes," he said, as if somebody had accused him of not doing it. "The cave is over there. When the thing came out and attacked Nicoletta, it came out of there."

"Nothing attacked me," said Nicoletta.

"It touched you," said Christo.

"There was nothing here," said Nicoletta.

"I believe you, Christo!" sang Anne-Louise. "I know there was something here. I'll go with you, Christo!"

Anne-Louise and Christo walked carefully as if they were on a balance beam. The water reached up to catch their ankles. A moment passed before Rachel and Cathy and David and Jeff walked after them. Did they not see the cliff snarl? Did they not see the hunger of the cave, how it licked its lips with wanting them?

"There *is* a cave!" cried Rachel. "Oh, Christo, you were right! Oh my heavens! Look inside. It's beautiful!"

No, thought Nicoletta. No, Rachel, it's not beautiful. Don't go in, don't go in.

But now her tongue was also plaster and did

not move, but filled her mouth and prevented her speech.

No one went in.

A cave gives pause. Even with walls shining like jewels, the dark depths are frightening and the unknown beyond the light should remain unknown.

The Madrigals posed at the entrance, as if waiting for their cue to sing, needing costumes, or a director to bring them in.

"Anne-Louise," said a voice, "you go first."

Chapter 19

The screams of Anne-Louise were etched in the air, like diamond initials on glass. Indeed, glass seemed to separate the safe from the fallen.

The Madrigals were collected as if about to concertize. But it was horror that held them, not an audience. They, in fact, were the audience. They had aisle seats to the end of Anne-Louise.

Anne-Louise, whose voice was not so beautiful when screaming in terror, was on the far side of the glass.

The screams went on and on and then stopped. They stopped completely. The silence that followed was even more complete.

Nobody attempted to go in after her.

Nobody tried to rescue her.

Were they too afraid? Or too smart to risk the same ending?

Nicoletta had the excuse of an immovable

leg, a helpless body. None of the others had an excuse.

But Nicoletta had known what would happen. None of the others could have known. And so Nicoletta Storms was the one with no excuse at all, no excuse ever.

Whose voice sent Anne-Louise tumbling forever into the dark?

Was it me? thought Nicoletta. Did I shout *Anne-Louise, you go first!* I who knew what would happen to the one who went first? Did I want revenge that much? How sick and twisted I am, to destroy a classmate over a singing group.

I'm sorry! thought Nicoletta. As if being sorry would change anything.

Time stopped.

The sun did not move in the sky and the teenagers did not move beneath it.

Sound ceased.

Nothing cried out within the cave and nobody spoke without.

The glass wall broke.

Anne-Louise, babbling and twitching, fingers curling and uncurling, eyes too wide to blink, staggered out of the cave.

Still nobody spoke. Still nobody moved.

They were like a group photograph of themselves. A still shot of Madrigals from another era.

"It's in there," whispered Anne-Louise. "You were right, Christo. It's in there! It picked me up. It caught me."

Anne-Louise addressed Christo but did not seem to see him. Instead she staggered away from the cliff, hands out as if holding a rope nobody else could see. On an invisible lifeline she hauled herself in Nicoletta's direction. There was sand in her hair, as if she were a bride at some dreadful wedding. Her guests had not thrown confetti.

"It's there?" breathed Christo. Excitement possessed him. "It really exists? You saw it? You touched it?"

"Don't go in!" screamed Anne-Louise. Her voice was huge and roiling, nothing like a soprano's. It was ugly and swollen. "Don't go in!" she shouted. She did not let go of her lifeline, but kept hauling herself between the lakes, past Nicoletta. She fell to her knees, and Nicoletta saw that the kneecaps were torn and bruised from an earlier fall. Still Anne-Louise did not stop, but crawled, sobbing, trying to find the straight path and the way out.

"She's right, Christo," said Rachel. She sounded quite normal. "Don't go in there. What we'll do is come back with a truck and ropes.

Obviously it's slippery and the cave falls off. There are people who go into caves for hobbies. I've read about them. They're called spelunkers. We'll get in touch with a club and bring a group that knows what they're doing. We'll — "

"No!" said Christo. "It's my find! I'm getting it!"

Jethro saved Anne-Louise, thought Nicoletta. She wanted to call *thank you!* to him. She wanted to shout *I love you!* in his direction. She wanted to put her arms around him and tell him that he was good and kind.

How many people had he saved in the past? Nicoletta had been horrified because Jethro let the hunters fall. But he hadn't let Nicoletta fall. He hadn't let Anne-Louise fall.

He would let Christo fall. He would have to.

"Fine," said Christo in the furious voice of one who means the opposite. "Fine! I'll take everybody back to the van. Fine! We'll picnic at the lake. And then I'm coming back and I'm getting it."

Anne-Louise was walking upright now, a stagger to her gait as if something in her had permanently snapped. Rachel and Cathy were running to catch up and help her. The rest of the Madrigals, saying little, crept between the lakes, safely away from the stretching black

173

elastic of the water, picked up the pace, and headed for the van.

For a moment, Nicoletta thought they would abandon her; that half the curse would come true. She prayed they would, because if she sat long enough, Jethro would come to her. Her Jethro. Jethro with the smooth quiet features, the heavy falling hair, the dark, motionless eyes.

But the boys remembered they had two burdens: a girl and a cooler. They hoisted her up, silently and with great tension, wanting to run, not wanting to admit it.

"You'll see, Nicoletta," said Christo eagerly. "I'll get it."

He wants "it" for me, she thought. "It" will be his trophy to lay at my feet, a golden retriever laying the gunshot duck before his master.

She knew now that Christo could never get "it." "It" would always win, because "it" had greater, deeper, more ancient and more horrible weapons.

She did not want Christo to fall, and not be saved.

She did not want Jethro to have to face that moment. To know that he could rescue . . . and would not.

She did not want coming here to be a hobby.

She did not want to think of the collection that would lie at the bottom of the cave. Or, if Jethro were caught on the outside, the collection he would be in, the display he would make.

The boys staggered in the snow, losing their footing.

Nicoletta looked back. The cliff face was nothing but rock and dripping ice. The lakes were nothing but dark surfaces. The hole in the wall was not visible.

And then part of the rock moved. Changed. Was light, and then dark. A dark wand rose upward. An arm. After a time in the air, like a flag without wind, the hand moved.

It was Jethro.

Terrible grief engulfed her. Was that his good-bye? Would she never see Jethro again? "Put me down!" she cried. "I have to go back!" Her heart was swept out of her, rushing like wind and desperation toward the last wave.

But the boys trudged on.

Chapter 20

Nobody would return anywhere that night.

The snow came down like a monster itself. It came in bulk, in dump-truck loads, smothering every car and bush and front step.

At least school would be canceled. At least Christo would be unable to get his van out of his driveway.

Long after Jamie had fallen asleep, Nicoletta raised the shades and sat up in bed, watching the beauty and the rage of the weather. The wind was not a single whooshing entity but a thousand tiny spinners. The night was dark with desperate clouds letting go, but yellow pools of streetlights illuminated the falling snow.

Jethro came.

She had not expected him. She had thought him gone forever. She had been in mourning, believing in his good-bye, sure that he had backed off for good.

"Jethro!" she cried, and then twisted quickly to see if she had awakened Jamie. Jamie slept on. She put a hand over her mouth to keep herself from speaking again.

When he moved, Nicoletta could see him. When he stopped, she could not. He was part of the landscape. He could have been a dark wind himself, or a heavy clot of snow on rock.

She looked at her sleeping sister. Jamie's mouth was slightly opened and in sleep she seemed glued to the sheets, fastened down by the blankets. She wouldn't wake unless Nicoletta fell right on top of her.

Nicoletta found her crutches, and slowly — far too slowly; what if Jethro left before she could get outside? — she made it down the stairs and reached the coat closet, wrapped herself tightly and hobbled to the back door to let herself out in the storm.

The wind aimed at her face. It threw pellets of ice in her eyes and tried to damage her bare cheeks. The three back steps could have been cliffs themselves. The distance between herself and the garage seemed like miles. "Jethro!" she shouted, but the wind reached into her throat first and seized the words.

"Jethro!"

Nobody could have heard her; she could not even hear herself.

She tried to wade through the snow but it was impossible. It would have been like swimming and the broken leg could not swim.

Why was he not at the door, waiting for her?

She gulped in snow, and put a hand blue with cold over her mouth. She should have worn mittens but she had expected to be out here only a moment before Jethro found her.

She launched the tip of her crutches into the snow ahead of her and attempted to get through the drifts.

There he was! By the garage door! She shouted his name twice, and he did not respond, and she shouted a third time, and he turned — or rather, it turned — and she waved the whole crutch in order to be seen.

He seemed to turn and to stoop. As if he were on an errand. Carrying something. When at last she knew Jethro had seen her, he looked away. What is this? thought Nicoletta. What is going on?

But she had been seeing things. Of course he came to her, white with snow. Snow purified and cleansed. Again he lifted her, and carried her this time into the garage, sitting her on the edge of her father's workbench, her good knee dangling down while the white plaster tip of her cast rested on the top of her mother's car. "You came," she said. "I knew you would come."

He said nothing.

For a frigid, suffocating moment she thought it was somebody else. Not Jethro. Some — creature — who —

She looked and at least knew his eyes: those dark pools of grief.

"Jethro, I don't want you to live like this."

"No," he agreed.

She could feel no pulse in him, no heartbeat, no lifting of a chest with lungs. He was stone beside her.

"You stay here and live. I will go down for you."

He did not smile, for there was no face to him that could do that. And yet he lightened and seemed glad. "No," he said again. The thing that was his hand tightened on hers.

"I don't want you to suffer anymore."

He said nothing.

"I've thought about it. It's your turn for life, Jethro. I will go down."

The words came as from a fissure in a rock. "No one should suffer what I have. Certainly not you."

"Aren't you even tempted? Aren't you even

daydreaming about what it would be like to be alive and well and normal and loved?"

"Always."

"Well?"

"Nicoletta, I will never be well and normal and loved."

"*I* love you!"

He was silent for a long time. The storm shrieked as it tried to fling the roof off the house. The snow whuffling into deepening drifts. "Thank you," he said finally.

"There won't be school tomorrow," she said.

He did not seem to know why.

"Canceled," she explained. "Snow is too deep."

He nodded.

Oh, tonight of all nights she did not want his silence! She wanted to talk! To know. To understand. To share. "When school begins again, will you be in Art?"

"No."

"Jethro, you have to come. Where else will I see you?"

His silence was longer than ever. She was determined to wait him out, to make him talk. She won. He said, "This is only pain and grief."

"What is?"

"Loving."

"You're wrong! It can end well! I want you to stay."

"Like this?" Bitterness conquered him. "Why would I want to be seen like this? What do you think will happen? Christo will exhibit me in a cage." He did not point out that if she had never come back to his cave, if she had never been followed by Christo, he would not be at risk. But they both knew it.

His voice rose like the wind, screaming with the pain of his nightmare. "I don't want anybody to see me. I didn't want you to see me!"

What would it be like, she wondered, to be so ghastly you did not even want the people who loved you to see you? What would it be like to look down at your own body and be nauseated? To be trapped — a fine soul; a good human — in such ugliness that another human would want to put you in a cage and exhibit you?

Nicoletta was freezing to death. It was not just Jethro's body in which she could feel no pulse, no heartbeat, no lungs. "I have to get inside," she said. "I'm so cold. I don't think I can move. Jethro, carry me inside?"

He said nothing, but lifted her. Her skin scraped against him and she hoped that it was deep, and would bleed, and leave a scar, so she would have something to remember him by.

He took her up the back steps and opened the door for her. He saw how she lived; the warmth and clutter, the letters and the photographs, the dishes and the chairs. The goodness of family and the rightness of life.

"I love you, too," he said, his voice cracking like old ice. "But try to see. I can't risk anything more, Nicoletta. You can't risk anything more. I can't be caught. I can't let Christo fall. He loves you. I care about anybody who loves you."

"You saved Anne-Louise," she said softly. "You're a good person. It isn't fair when somebody good suffers! Let me rescue you. I know there must be a way out of this."

His voice was oddly generous, as if he were giving her something. "When your leg is better," he said, "come to the cave. But don't come before that. Promise me. I need your promise."

"No."

"Nicoletta! Why won't you promise?"

"I love you. I want to see you."

"Don't come." He set her down. The one side of her was flooded with the warmth of her home and its furnace. The other side was crusted with snow turning to sleet.

She began arguing with him. Reasons why she must come, why they must get together, why they needed each other, and could think of some way somehow to save each other, because that was what true love did; it conquered, it triumphed.

She thought it was a wonderful speech.

She knew that she had changed his mind, that he understood because she had said it so clearly.

But when she put her hand out, there was nothing there.

A snowdrift pressed against the door and a snow-clumped branch from a heavy-laden fir tree tipped over the railing and tried to reach inside the kitchen. But no boy, no monster, no rock.

No Jethro.

He had left her, and she had not even sensed it.

He had gone, and she had not even heard.

"No!" she shouted out into the snow. "Who do you think you are anyway? Don't you vanish like that!"

Only the snow answered.

Only the wind heard.

"I don't promise, Jethro!" she shrieked.

The side door to the garage banged.

Jethro had not come to see her. She had been right when she thought he stooped and carried. He had come for the dynamite.

Tears froze on her cheeks but hope was resurrected. He had thought of a way out. He was going to use one of her suggestions. He would blow up the cave, and bury the curse, and when she came back to find him, they would be together!

Chapter 21

"Nicoletta, darling," said Ms. Quincy.

Nicoletta turned away, saw who was speaking, and very nearly continued on. How she yearned to be rude to the teacher she had once adored. She looked now at Ms. Quincy and saw not a friend, but a conductor who set friendship aside if she could improve the concert by doing so.

Nicoletta did not even know what was fair, let alone what was right.

In fairness, should the best soprano win? Or in fairness, should the hard-working, long-term soprano stay?

What was right? What was good teaching? What was good music?

Were the concert, the blend, the voices always first, and rightly so?

Or did loyalty, friendship, and committee time count?

She wondered if Ms. Quincy had wondered about these things, or if Ms. Quincy, like so many adults, was sure of her way? When she became an adult, would Nicoletta know the way?

She thought of Jethro, who knew the way but could not take it.

Of Jethro's father, who knew the way once but lost the memory of it.

Of Art Appreciation and Jethro's empty chair.

She said, "Hello, Ms. Quincy, how are you?" Manners were important. You always had them to go by. When you stood to lose all else, there were still manners.

"Fine, thank you, darling," said Ms. Quincy, relieved that Nicoletta was going to be polite.

Politeness is a safety zone, thought Nicoletta. She thought of Jethro coming out of her garage. The dynamite that no longer lay in the box on the shelf. Had he done what he had set out to do? She must go! She must see what had happened. She must find him and know.

Practically speaking, this meant she would have to get a ride from somebody. Who?

"Anne-Louise," said Ms. Quincy, "has let me down."

Down, thought Nicoletta. You have no idea,

Ms. Quincy, what the word *down* means to Anne-Louise now. You have no idea how far down Anne-Louise actually went. "I'm sorry to hear that," said Nicoletta politely. "But I'm sure it will work out in the end."

"No, darling. She has quit Madrigals! Can you believe such a thing?" Clearly Ms. Quincy could not. "And here we are in the middle of the winter season with several upcoming events!" Ms. Quincy was actually wringing her hands, an interesting gesture Nicoletta had never seen anybody do. "Nicoletta, please forgive me. Please come back. We need you."

Back to Madrigals.

Back in the group she loved, in the center of things, the whirl of activity and companionship and singing. Back, if she chose, as Christo's girlfriend, twice the center of things with that status.

But never . . . if she rejoined Madrigals . . . never again to sit in Art Appreciation. Waiting. Gazing on the boy she loved.

She knew Jethro was not coming back to school. He had said so quite clearly. And yet she knew she would see him again. She had to. A person you loved could not simply never be seen again. It was not fair.

In the end, things — especially things of true love — should be fair.

Three days of school since the roads were finally cleared, and each afternoon as she went to Art, her heart quickened, and a smile lay behind her lips. Let him come! Let me see that profile. The boy who was in darkness when they watched slides and remained dark when the lights came on.

He did not come.

If she did not continue in Art Appreciation, she would never know if he came back. If she did not rejoin Madrigals, she could not gather back those friendships and pleasures either. "I'll think about it, Ms. Quincy."

It had never occurred to the woman that Nicoletta might say no. There was a certain revenge in seeing Ms. Quincy's shock. "Nicoletta," said Ms. Quincy severely, "you are cutting off your nose to spite your face."

Nicoletta had never heard that saying before and had to consider it.

"You will hurt yourself more than you will hurt the group," said Ms. Quincy, putting it another way.

Nicoletta wondered if that was true. "I'll let you know on Monday, Ms. Quincy," said Nicoletta. "First I'll talk to Anne-Louise."

Anne-Louise was fully recovered. In fact, she was laughing about it. "I can't believe how

I behaved," she said. "Isn't it funny?"

If it's so funny, thought Nicoletta, why did you quit Madrigals?

"You know what let's do?" said Anne-Louise.

"What?"

"Let's go back to the cave," said Anne-Louise. "I mean, when I got home the other day, my mother said my eyes were glazed over. She thought I had cataracts or something. My mother said, 'Anne-Louise, what happened out there anyway?' And do you know what, Nicoletta?"

"What?"

"I can't remember exactly what happened. Let's go back and see. I'm curious. I don't understand what scared us all so much. It was only a cave."

"It's more than a cave. It needs victims," said Nicoletta. "You must not go back. You must never go back, Anne-Louise."

Anne-Louise shrugged. "I'm going back to the cave now, Nicoletta. I *have* to see it," said Anne-Louise. "Do you want to come?"

What way out, thought Nicoletta, would preserve us all? What way out saves Jethro, but gives him to me? Keeps us from exploring or falling? Gives Jethro life as a boy and not a monster?

But did it matter anymore? She thought she knew what way Jethro had decided would work.

No way.

The snow was so high it covered the DEAD END sign. The trees were like branch children with snow blankets pulled up to their shoulders.

Anne-Louise's car reached the end of the road. Here the immense amount of snow had been piled by the plows into sheer-sided mountains. The path was not visible. There was no way in to the boulder.

The road, indeed, was a dead end.

The girls got out of the car. Nicoletta had learned how to use her cast; it was just a heavier, more annoying leg than she had had before. She did not need the crutches for pain or balance.

They surveyed the problem. The snow was taller than they were. Shovels, possibly pick axes, would be necessary to break through. And beyond the snow-plowed mountains, it would still be nearly up to Nicoletta's waist. There was more snow here than elsewhere, as if the snow had conspired to conceal the path until spring.

Anne-Louise looked confused. She rattled

her car keys. She was losing touch with what she wanted to do, and thinking of leaving.

Yes, leave! thought Nicoletta. Leave me here. I'll get to him somehow; I know I will, because he needs me and I need him. He can't have left me forever. Jethro! she called through her heart and her mind. I'm coming!

Christo pulled in behind them. Oh, Christo, why do you always show up, as if I cared about you? she thought.

But he kissed her, because he knew nothing. "We'll just go around," he said.

She had never thought of that; never thought of just walking back to where the plows had not packed the snow so high. Christo went first, kicking a path. Anne-Louise went second, widening the path.

Nicoletta went third, dragging her cast.

The boulder had never seemed so huge. Snow had fallen from the surrounding trees, pitting the soft layers on the boulder. It looked volcanic, as if seething hot lava was bubbling just beneath the snow, waiting for them to put out a wrong foot.

But only to Nicoletta's eyes. To Christo they seemed the right places to step, where the snow was dented. He slogged forward, a football player with a goal in mind. A camera swung from his shoulder.

Nicoletta thought of the order in which they were going. Victims at the head of the line. "Stop," she said. "Stop, Christo!" It's dangerous for them, she thought. But not for me. Love will save me. Love always triumphs. I know it does! Jethro will save me, and we will be together.

"Nickie, I'm never stopping," said Christo. "I'm going to figure out what's happening here if it kills me."

The boulder moved.

It rolled right in front of them. The ground began to shake. Nicoletta had never known how terrible, how awe-full an earthquake is. Nothing in life was so dependable as the ground under her feet. Now it tossed her off, as if she were going to have to fly; she could no longer stand, the old order of human beings was ended.

Anne-Louise's scream pierced the sky, but the sky cared nothing for humans without sense and her scream flattened to nothing under the gray ceiling.

The stone rolled onto Christo's ankle and pinned him.

A huge and terrible noise came from beyond; greater noise than Nicoletta had ever heard; a shattering of rock and earth deeper than man had ever mined. Jethro had dynamited the entrance to the cave.

And then, and only then, Nicoletta knew what way out Jethro had thought of. Not one of hers. But his own.

For there was no way out that preserved them all.

Nicoletta was right that love triumphs. Jethro loved her. And he had put that first. He loved her enough to prevent her from coming back, from bringing her friends, from risking their lives.

He had closed his door forever. Himself inside.

They will all be buried this time, she thought. Every sorrowful spirit will find its rest. Buried at last. *Including Jethro.*

The shaking dashed Nicoletta against a tree.

Jethro gave me life, she thought. For the second time in his terrible life, he sacrificed himself for the person he loved. He wanted me to have my life: sharing a bedroom with a little sister, singing in Madrigals, and eating in the cafeteria.

He wanted no more hunters falling, no more Christos, no more Anne-Louises. He did not want me to risk myself again. He did not want another person on this earth to abandon, or to be abandoned.

Jethro. I love you.

The earth ceased its leaping. The stone rolled off Christo. He was only bruised. He got up easily.

The path through the meadow had received no snow. It was clear as a summer day, straight as the edge of a page. Christo and Anne-Louise led the way, Nicoletta following, her good leg walking and the other leg dragging.

There was no rock face left. There were no ponds. A jumble of fallen stone and rock lay where once a tall cliff and two circles of water had been.

"Wow," said Christo reverently, and lifted his camera. He got into camera athletics, squatting and whirling and arching for the best angle.

Nothing else moved.

Not a rock. Not a stone. Not a crystal.

"I didn't abandon you, Jethro," whispered Nicoletta. "I want you to know that. I came this afternoon to find you. So we could be together after all. I didn't know this was your plan. I swear I didn't. I thought you were only going to bury *them*."

There was only silence. The rocks that had made such a tremendous crash had made the only sound they ever would. They were done with motion and noise. And Jethro? Was he, too, done with motion and noise?

Jethro. I love you.

"Wow!" Christo kept saying. He bounded from rock to rock. "What do you think set it off? Was it an earthquake? I never heard of earthquakes in this part of the country. Wow!"

It was my father's dynamite, thought Nicoletta. But it was Jethro's courage.

Are you well and truly buried now, Jethro? Is the curse over? Are you safe in heaven?

Or deep within this cruel earth, are you still there? Your upward path closed? Still in the dark, forever and ever caught with the raging undead? Never again to hear laughter? Never again to hold a hand?

Oh, Jethro, I hope what you did for me worked for you, too!

I love you. Jethro! Be safe!

Christo finished the roll of film. "Let's go home," he said. "I want to call the television studio. The newspapers. I think my science teachers would love to see this, too."

Love, love, love. How Christo had misspelled that precious word. Only Nicolette knew what love was. And only Jethro had shown it.

"Jethro!" she screamed then. It was too much to keep inside herself. *"Jethro!"* she shrieked, trying to explode his spirit as the dynamite had exploded the rocks. She tried to run toward him, or where he had been, tried to find the place from which he had waved, his stone arm lifted to say farewell.

But of course she could not move, for the cast kept her in place, and the broken, destroyed surface of the earth presented a thousand rocky obstacles. "Jethro!" she screamed. "Jethro!"

She hated silence. How dare Jethro be silent? She wanted him to answer! She wanted him to speak!

Her tears spilled down her face and fell on her pleading hands.

It seemed to her as she wept, that the tears were full of sand, not salt, and that when they dried on her hands, she had some of Jethro in her palm.

"Be safe!" she cried. "Be at rest! Oh, Jethro, be safe!"

Christo said, "What are you talking about?" He shepherded the two girls toward the van.

Talking? thought Nicoletta. I am trying to be heard through hundreds of years of abandonment, and through thousands of tons of rock. I am screaming! I am screaming for the soul of a boy who loved me.

Anne-Louise rattled her car keys.

Christo rewound his film.

They reached the boulder. Nicoletta rested her hand on the snowcap it wore. There was nothing. Snow. Rock. Solidity. She put the same hand on her heart. It was as cracked as crystal thrown from the cliff. And no one knew, or heard.

"Jethro," she whispered.

It seemed to her that for a tender moment, the frozen trees of the woods, the lakes and ledges and stones of the earth, bent toward her and understood her sorrow.

Christo opened the van door for Nicoletta, and boosted her in. "Where does that Jethro kid live anyway?"

She looked into the silent woods and thought of Jethro, silent forever. "He moved," said Nicoletta. Let it be true, she prayed. Let him be safe wherever he moved to, wherever he lies.

Jethro, it was too much. To die for me was too much. I wanted you alive! I wanted us together! You can't do that with death. With death you can't be together.

Christo started the engine.

She looked down at her hand. Caught in the tiny cup of her curved palm was a grain of sand glittering like a diamond. She closed her fingers to keep her diamond safe. The way, with his death, Jethro had kept her safe.

They left in the little lane with its dwindling

ruts, and the trees closed around the road as if it had never been.

Her breath was hot in the icy van. It clouded the window. With the hand that held no diamond, she traced a heart in the mist on the glass. She wrote no initials within the heart, for she did not know Jethro's, and Christo would expect his initials to go beside hers.

They drove on, and the van heated up, and the warm air erased the heart.

But Jethro would not be erased. Jethro had lived and loved. He had loved *her*. Nicoletta Storms opened her hand. The diamond lay still and silent in her palm.

And always would.

About the Author

Caroline B. Cooney lives in a small seacoast village in Connecticut. She writes every day on a word processor and then goes for a long walk down the beach to figure out what she's going to write the following day. She's written fifty books for young people. *The Fog*, *The Snow*, and *The Fire* was her first horror series, followed by another series, *The Cheerleader*, *The Return of the Vampire*, and *The Vampire's Promise*. Her other thrillers include *The Perfume* and *Freeze Tag*. She reads as much as possible and has three grown children.

THRILLERS

R.L. Stine

- ☐ MC44236-8 The Baby-sitter — $3.50
- ☐ MC44332-1 The Baby-sitter II — $3.50
- ☐ MC46099-4 The Baby-sitter III — $3.50
- ☐ MC45386-6 Beach House — $3.25
- ☐ MC43278-8 Beach Party — $3.50
- ☐ MC43125-0 Blind Date — $3.50
- ☐ MC43279-6 The Boyfriend — $3.50
- ☐ MC44333-X The Girlfriend — $3.50
- ☐ MC45385-8 Hit and Run — $3.25
- ☐ MC46100-1 The Hitchhiker — $3.50
- ☐ MC43280-X The Snowman — $3.50
- ☐ MC43139-0 Twisted — $3.50

Caroline B. Cooney

- ☐ MC44316-X The Cheerleader — $3.25
- ☐ MC41641-3 The Fire — $3.25
- ☐ MC43806-9 The Fog — $3.25
- ☐ MC45681-4 Freeze Tag — $3.25
- ☐ MC45402-1 The Perfume — $3.25
- ☐ MC44884-6 The Return of the Vampire — $2.95
- ☐ MC41640-5 The Snow — $3.25
- ☐ MC45682-2 The Vampire's Promise — $3.50

Diane Hoh

- ☐ MC44330-5 The Accident — $3.25
- ☐ MC45401-3 The Fever — $3.25
- ☐ MC43050-5 Funhouse — $3.25
- ☐ MC44904-4 The Invitation — $3.50
- ☐ MC45640-7 The Train — $3.25

Sinclair Smith

- ☐ MC45063-8 The Waitress — $2.95

Christopher Pike

- ☐ MC43014-9 Slumber Party — $3.50
- ☐ MC44256-2 Weekend — $3.50

A. Bates

- ☐ MC45829-9 The Dead Game — $3.25
- ☐ MC43291-5 Final Exam — $3.25
- ☐ MC44582-0 Mother's Helper — $3.50
- ☐ MC44238-4 Party Line — $3.25

D.E. Athkins

- ☐ MC45246-0 Mirror, Mirror — $3.25
- ☐ MC45349-1 The Ripper — $3.25
- ☐ MC44941-9 Sister Dearest — $2.95

Carol Ellis

- ☐ MC46411-6 Camp Fear — $3.25
- ☐ MC44768-8 My Secret Admirer — $3.25
- ☐ MC46044-7 The Stepdaughter — $3.25
- ☐ MC44916-8 The Window — $2.95

Richie Tankersley Cusick

- ☐ MC43115-3 April Fools — $3.25
- ☐ MC43203-6 The Lifeguard — $3.25
- ☐ MC43114-5 Teacher's Pet — $3.25
- ☐ MC44235-X Trick or Treat — $3.25

Lael Littke

- ☐ MC44237-6 Prom Dress — $3.25

Edited by T. Pines

- ☐ MC45256-8 Thirteen — $3.50

Available wherever you buy books, or use this order form.

Scholastic Inc., P.O. Box 7502, 2931 East McCarty Street, Jefferson City, MO 65102

Please send me the books I have checked above. I am enclosing $_____ (please add $2.00 to cover shipping and handling). Send check or money order — no cash or C.O.D.s please.

Name _____ Birthdate _____

Address_____

City_____ State/Zip_____

Please allow four to six weeks for delivery. Offer good in the U.S. only. Sorry, mail orders are not available to residents of Canada. Prices subject to change.

T193